> ## "Why'd you agree to this marriage when you didn't wish it?"

She knew how right she was when he stiffened. "Look, sweetheart, I just wasn't sure we could get along. But now we don't have any doubt about our being compatible, do we?" He touched a finger against her lips, as if to emphasize his point.

"But why marry me if you didn't know me?" she pressed.

Pete told her about his mother's plan. "She'd sell this ranch out from under me in a New York minute."

All Liz's dreams of convincing him he loved her instead of the real princess faded into the night. She might be able to compete against a blue blood, but she had no chance against Pete's beloved Montana ranch.

Pete took her chin between his thumb and forefinger and lifted her face to his. "We each have our reasons for this marriage. And maybe we'll find a few more. Not the least of which is this."

Sweetly, seductively, he covered her lips with his....

ABOUT THE AUTHOR

Before turning to contemporary romance, Judy Christenberry wrote Regency romances for twelve years. She burst upon the American Romance scene in 1994 and has quickly become a reader favorite. After having taught high-school French for many years, Judy now writes full-time. The mother of two grown daughters, she makes her home in Texas, which is why she writes such good cowboys!

Be sure to catch the continuing adventures of Pete Morris and his brother Robert in American Romance #735, MY DADDY THE DUKE, coming in July.

Books by Judy Christenberry

HARLEQUIN AMERICAN ROMANCE

555—FINDING DADDY
579—WHO'S THE DADDY?
612—WANTED: CHRISTMAS MOMMY
626—DADDY ON DEMAND
649—COWBOY CUPID*
653—COWBOY DADDY*
661—COWBOY GROOM*
665—COWBOY SURRENDER*
701—IN PAPA BEAR'S BED

*4 Brides for 4 Brothers

A Cowboy
at Heart

JUDY CHRISTENBERRY

Harlequin Books

TORONTO • NEW YORK • LONDON
AMSTERDAM • PARIS • SYDNEY • HAMBURG
STOCKHOLM • ATHENS • TOKYO • MILAN
MADRID • WARSAW • BUDAPEST • AUCKLAND

ISBN 0-373-16726-1

A COWBOY AT HEART

Copyright © 1998 by Judy Christenberry.

Prologue

Liz Caine slid into the room, completely comfortable with the stares of the two men. After all, her looks were part of the job.

A swift intake of breath from one of her observers was a compliment. She smiled.

"The eyes. The princess has green eyes."

"No problem. Contacts will cure that," Georgia, her friend and the owner of Georgia's Lookalikes, assured the man.

The other man, the one who hadn't spoken, began to circle Liz, slowly studying her from every angle. "Incredible," he muttered as if to himself. "She will be perfect."

Liz waited, but when none of the three added any details, she asked, "Perfect for what?"

Georgia moved to her side. "Perfect to pretend to be a princess. Won't that be fun?"

Liz wasn't sure about the fun part. She'd worked for Georgia to keep food on the table while she sought fame and fortune in Hollywood. But she'd finally realized Hollywood wasn't where she belonged.

She was about to return home to Kansas, to her recently widowed mother. To a simpler life, where honesty was the rule, not the exception as it was here in Hollywood. But Georgia had called yesterday with a desperate plea for her help. And an offer of a lot of money.

Liz's dad had been a sweetheart, a veterinarian with a heart of gold. He'd given to any hand held out, shared with strangers, donated to charities and worked on people's animals for free. When a heart attack took him four months ago, his widow discovered that his generosity to others had left her in bad shape financially.

The idea that by working one last job for Georgia Liz could earn some extra money to help out her mom had made easy her decision to postpone her return by a day or two.

"What do I have to do?" Liz asked, looking at the two men. It bothered her when they exchanged a look before answering her question.

"The princess is scheduled to spend some time on a ranch in Montana. She is concerned about the publicity. She is constantly hounded by the press," the shorter man explained with an ingratiating smile.

Liz smiled back. The two men reminded her of the old cartoon characters, Mutt and Jeff. One was tall and spare, the other short and round.

"So you want me to go to the ranch in her place?" she asked. "That's it?" It sounded too good to be true.

Again the men exchanged looks. "Yes, of course," the tall one finally said.

"And what will the real princess be doing?" she asked, curiosity filling her.

The shorter man shifted from foot to foot. "Uh, the Princess will be…"

"Incognito," the tall man interjected. "Somewhere safe and secure and solitary." He smiled, as if pleased.

"How much time will you need me?"

"Only a week. Then the princess is scheduled to return to her homeland."

"And she'll never see these people again?"

"Not for a number of months. Enough time for them to have forgotten any particulars about her."

"I hadn't planned on a week. Couldn't we make it a shorter visit?" She really was anxious to go home. Her mother's last phone call had sounded so forlorn.

"They're offering a handsome fee," Georgia reminded her, leaning close so she wouldn't be overheard.

"How handsome?" Liz whispered. Georgia hadn't yet mentioned specific details.

"A hundred thousand."

Liz blinked several times in surprise, then she beamed at the two men.

"I'm your princess," she agreed with a curtsy.

Chapter One

"Are we gonna have to curtsy every time this here princess bumps into us?" Harvey, a longtime employee on the Palisades Ranch, demanded, glaring at his boss.

Lord Peter Morris, second in line to a dukedom in England, grinned at the grizzled employee. Harvey, bow-legged and bald, had been on Pete's grandfather's ranch as long as he could remember. "I think I should say yes just to see you curtsy."

Several of the other cowboys laughed.

"Well, I reckon I'd do a better job of it than Will," Harvey returned, naming one of his companions.

Before an argument could break out, Pete raised his hand. "None of you has to curtsy to Princess Elsbeth. After all, this is America. If she's going to marry me, she'll have to adjust to life on a ranch."

"If? You mean it isn't a done deal? Your grandpa must be turnin' over in his grave to even think of you marryin' some snooty foreigner."

Pete sighed and turned away, muttering, "It's a

done deal, Harvey. You boys hit the saddle. I've got some business to take care of up at the house.''

Pete walked out of the barn into the brilliant sunshine of a Montana summer. Normally he'd delight in his surroundings, but today, with the arrival of his fiancée imminent, he scarcely noticed the beauty.

Fiancée. Hah! Strange word for a woman he'd met only twice for a total of about half an hour. Had he made the right decision?

Hell, it was too late to back out now. He'd given his mother his word. Females! His mother had known exactly how to persuade him. She'd offered the deed to his beloved ranch, twenty-five thousand acres of prime Montana land.

All he had to do was marry Princess Elsbeth from the small country of Cargenia in central Europe.

His boots sounded on the planks of the porch as he crossed it to the back door of the main house. Stepping into the cool shade of the kitchen, he headed for the coffeepot.

''Any calls, Maisie?''

''Them foreign gentlemen called. Said they'd be here on schedule.'' His housekeeper never looked up from the bowl she was working over.

''That means we'll have company for the next week. Everything ready?''

The look of disgust she cast him made an impression. He leaned forward and kissed her weathered cheek. ''Sorry. Of course you have everything ready. I'll be in the office.''

''Wait.'' She took down a saucer, placed several

cookies on it and handed it to him. "To go with your coffee."

"Thanks, Maisie," he said, knowing the cookies were a peace offering.

When he reached the room he used as an office, he set the cookies and coffee down on the desk and began pacing the rug-covered floor. Damn, he must've been out of his head when he'd agreed to his mother's proposition.

He loved the ranch of course. From the time he'd first visited as a young lad, he'd been in love with the place. His mother had been raised on the ranch and yet she'd had no difficulty turning her back on her heritage once she'd met his father, the Duke of Hereford. Now she was more English than anyone born there.

As if thinking of her had brought it about, the phone rang, and his mother's voice, fake English accent and all, filled his ear. "Darling boy, has she arrived?"

Determined to be as perverse as possible, he asked, "Who, Mother?"

"Darling boy, I do wish you'd call me Mummy. Mother seems so...so formal."

"I'm a grown man, Mother."

"A grown man soon to own twenty-five thousand acres. Right, darling?"

He sighed. "I hope to own the ranch. Why can't we come to terms? I'd be able to make payments each month."

"Darling, that's so...so common. Besides, when you marry Princess Elsbeth, I'll need to give you a wedding present, and the ranch seems such a lovely one.''

While the dowager duchess had given up convincing her second son to return to England, she hadn't abandoned her desire to see him marry royalty. She'd even threatened to sell the ranch she'd inherited from her father last year out from under Pete if he didn't cooperate with her latest plan.

So he'd agreed.

''Mother, I don't want to marry royalty.''

''Why not? Just think—Prince Peter. What a lovely ring those words have.''

''How's Robert?'' he asked abruptly.

''Fine. Why do you ask?'' Her words didn't fool him. There was a stiffness in her voice that told him she knew why he'd asked that question.

''Don't you feel guilty?''

''Of course not. Celia is a lovely gel, quite well trained in her duties.''

''Too bad she isn't well trained in pleasing Robert.''

''Your brother expects too much.''

Pete released a deep sigh. ''He only expects what you and Father shared.''

''That's unfair,'' his mother responded with a sniff, making him feel lower than low. ''I must go to the vicar's for a committee meeting. Be kind to the princess.''

Before he could protest, she'd hung up.

Damn! In spite of her irritating ways, he loved his mother and hadn't intended to hurt her. Maybe that was part of what had gotten him in this mess.

He'd agreed to her scheming because he'd so badly wanted the ranch. Then he'd promptly put the agreement from his mind, hoping, he supposed, she wouldn't be able to pull the union off. Marriage wasn't something he looked forward to. Not after seeing his brother's experience.

But in a few hours Princess Elsbeth—his future wife—was due to arrive at the ranch. It was time he devised a plan.

His best hope was that the princess would refuse the marriage. His mother might even deed the ranch to him as compensation for his supposed heartbreak. Provided he was any good at acting.

He stopped to stare out the window at the rolling land, the distant mountain peaks, the grazing cattle. This was his life. From the time he was eight, he'd spent every summer here learning at his grandfather's knee. As soon as he'd finished the public school in England his mother had insisted he attend, he'd applied to the University of Montana.

His father had understood his fascination with life on the ranch. His mother hadn't.

His brother, Robert, the current Duke of Hereford and head of the family, had advised him to do what made him happy. So, in spite of his mother's protests, he'd returned to the ranch after his father's funeral. When his grandfather had died only a year later, Pete ran the cattle operation for his mother.

At least he would until this matchmaking failed.

Poor Robert had already been snared by his mother's plotting. Six months ago he'd married an earl's daughter, Celia, now the Duchess of Hereford.

From what Pete could determine, his brother was utterly miserable.

The woman was a cold fish, disinterested in his brother but not in his fortune. Damned if he, Pete, was going to fall into the same trap!

Half an hour later he passed through the kitchen again on his way to the back door.

Maisie glanced his way and then froze, staring at him. "What are you up to, Pete?"

He shrugged. "What do you mean, Maisie?"

"Those are the old clothes you wore for Halloween last year when you dressed as a bum. They're all torn and ugly."

"I'm going to do some dirty work. Didn't want to mess up my good clothes."

"But that princess is going to arrive in an hour. You be sure you get back here and change. We don't want her thinking you're uncivilized."

"Why, of course, Maisie."

He figured he'd make it back about the time the princess arrived. What he remembered about her was that she was a woman with a delicate nature and finicky taste, and was absolutely sanitized. He figured a couple hours of shoveling manure with the sloppiness of a first-timer ought to give him a fragrant appeal.

A grin spread across his face. Yeah. He'd have a lot of sex appeal for a woman who never moved a foot without someone smoothing the way.

"BUT YOU HAVEN'T TOLD ME anything about the people I'm visiting," Liz protested as her two escorts closed their briefcases and fastened their seat belts.

They'd spent the past three hours drilling her on protocol and aspects of the princess's behavior. Behavior that made Liz think the princess was a snob of the highest order.

"They do not matter," Dansky said, looking out the window of the private jet.

"Not matter? They're going to be my hosts for a week and they don't matter?"

"You must remember it is a privilege to have you visit them," Petrocelli reminded her. He was the short round escort and Liz had already discovered he was the more approachable. Dansky was stiff and formal.

"Why is the princess going to Montana if she doesn't think it will be pleasant?" Somehow, Liz didn't believe she was getting the entire story.

"She promised her father." Dansky continued to stare out the window, but at least he was listening.

"But she's not keeping her promise."

"You are keeping her promise for her," Petrocelli said, as if explaining the basics to a child.

"I know, but—"

"All you must do is remain distant, keep apart from these people. Your Highness does not indulge in common activities."

"Common activities? What does that mean?"

"You will not care to visit the countryside nor indulge in local activities."

"And you must remember to avoid being private with anyone," Dansky added.

"Why?"

"Because that is not appropriate. We will remain

with you at all times," Petrocelli assured her pleasantly.

"You think I'll forget my role?"

"Americans do not show proper respect for royalty, Your Highness. We do not want you to be offended."

"If I can't be with people and I can't be alone with anyone," Liz asked, "then what will I do for a week?"

"Nothing," Dansky replied. "That is what Your Highness does best."

Just then the plane began its descent and Liz gave up her line of questioning. She'd just have to adjust to a dull week, isolated by her two guardians. The hundred thousand dollars already sitting in her mother's bank would make such boredom well worth it.

"HEY, JOSEPH, I've got an early Christmas present for you," Pete called out as he stepped into the barn.

The old cowpoke who tended the horses was just starting to clean the stalls. "Christmas? You crazy, boy? It's June, not December."

Pete chuckled. "I said it was early."

"What's this here present?"

Pete tossed the old man an orange. "Here. Sit down and eat this. I'm going to do your job for you."

"You got nothing better to do than shovel manure?"

"Absolutely nothing."

With unusual formality Joseph presented Pete with

his shovel and pitchfork and sat down on a bale of hay.

PETE HAD WORKED UP a healthy sweat, which, combined with the odor of manure on his boots and jeans, made for a distinct aroma by the time the phone in the barn rang.

Joseph rose from his bale of hay and answered it. "For you. It's Maisie," he said, holding out the receiver.

"Yeah, Maisie?"

"They're here!" Maisie whispered hoarsely. "Sneak in and head for the shower. I'll cover for you."

He hung up the phone and entered the one stall with an occupant. "Hold still, Sallie Mae," he muttered, and turned his back to the horse, rubbing against her.

"Hell, what are you doin'?" Henry asked, staring at him as if he was crazy.

"Adding a little perfume for a lady."

"Ladies don't like the smell of horses. You know Maisie won't let you sit down to eat if you're reeking of the barn."

Pete smiled and handed Henry back his shovel. "I'm hoping everything will be taken care of by the time dinner rolls around. Thanks, Henry."

"No problem," the old stablehand muttered, staring after him as he left the barn.

"No problem," Pete muttered to himself as he covered the distance between the barn and the big house. He only hoped his plan worked. He intended to offend the princess every way possible and have her running for the nearest airport before sundown.

Knowing Maisie would've put their guests in the front parlor, a room seldom used, he strode down the long hall to the front of the house, ignoring the back stairs that would've given him access to his room and bath.

Opening the door, he watched as Maisie served tea to the three visitors encased on the matching silken love seat and sofa. He felt a moment's chagrin at the sight of his grandfather's silver tea service, gleaming in the sunlight coming through the front window.

Maisie had gone to a lot of trouble for the fiasco about to follow.

"Howdy, folks!" he boomed, intentionally raising his voice.

Maisie spun around, horror on her face.

Pete's gaze left her and traveled to the only other female in the room. Princess Elsbeth. Only daughter of the King of Cargenia. The woman who would, much to his mother's happiness, bestow on him the title of prince and eventually king.

"Howdy, Beth," he boomed, and approached her with a silly grin on his face that widened at her startled expression. At their earlier brief meetings, he'd been all that was proper. While she was as good-looking as he remembered, she was as stiff and cold as his brother's wife.

The two men seated beside her immediately stood. One of them stepped in front of the princess, holding out his hand. "This is the Princess Elsbeth, my lord."

"That's what I said. Beth." He adroitly stepped

around the man, taking him by surprise. With his dirty hands he seized the princess's arms, covered in silk, and lifted her to her feet.

Crushing her to him, he covered her startled lips with his and kissed the living daylights out of her.

DEAR GOD, what have I gotten myself into?

Liz had been kissed before. But never like this. The cowboy who'd appeared so suddenly was big, strong, sexy...and smelled of the barn.

When he pulled back, her nose wrinkled unconsciously at his fragrant scent. But mostly she struggled to deal with the effect his lips had had on her.

"What's the matter, darlin'?" he asked, seemingly concerned by her response. "Don't you like me?"

Liz had a soft heart, something she'd inherited from her father. Any sob story had her digging in her pocket to share whatever she had. Lord Peter Morris's words evoked a natural reaction, the rush to reassure him—until she saw the unholy gleam in his brown eyes.

Glancing down at the stains on her blue silk suit, she pulled out of his hold and stepped back. "You surprised me," she said softly, checking her escorts' reaction to the cowboy out of the corner of her eye.

"I did? I figured you'd expect a kiss or two," the cowboy drawled.

He tugged her toward him again, but this time she resisted. Something wasn't kosher—or her guardians had misled her.

Dansky interrupted. "My lord, I don't believe the princess is— She didn't expect—"

She sure as heck hadn't, Liz agreed. These two autocrats beside her had assured her that the visit was a formality. That she'd be left alone to hide in her room.

"Who are you?" the cowboy demanded.

"Dansky, my lord. And this is Petrocelli. We are the King's emissaries traveling with the princess."

The gleam had gone from his eyes and his jaw firmed. "Well, let's get something straight, Dansky. What goes on between Beth and me is private. Stay out of it."

Either her escorts had lied to her, or Lord Peter Morris was changing the rules. And how the second son of a duke looked like a typical American cowboy—with a Western drawl that sounded real to her— she didn't know. Unless he was the second son of John "the Duke" Wayne.

Her meandering thoughts should've been turned to her reaction, because before she could think of anything to say, the cowboy had grabbed her hand and was headed out the door.

"Wait!" she cried, but he ignored her. Turning her head, she shot a panicked look at the other two men.

"My lord!" Dansky protested.

The cowboy kept going, with her trailing behind him like a calf on a rope.

"Wh-where are we going?" she got out as they moved down a long hall.

"We're taking a tour of your new home, darlin'," he roared, glee in his voice. "You're gonna love it!"

A tour? Of her "new home"? Why would the cowboy think this was her new home? She was only supposed to be here a week. Okay, she could deal with a tour. Then she intended to have a serious chat with the men who'd hired her.

"After all," the cowboy continued, "since we'll be marryin' real soon, you've got to feel comfortable here."

She stared at him, her feet refusing to work. *Marrying? Real soon?* She cast another frantic look at the men behind her. Oh, yeah. They were going to have a *very* serious chat.

Chapter Two

Pete was confused.

He intended to scare the woman away. Get rid of her. Convince her she wanted no part of him.

And he was doing a good job if her expression was anything to go by.

So why did he want to kiss her again?

He wasn't an inexperienced sixteen-year-old, head over heels in love with the first female he'd ever touched. At thirty-two, he was cynical, tired of women who pursued him for his title, his wealth or even his body. He wanted no part of a marriage of convenience, sold to his mother's ambition.

But he still wanted to kiss her again.

They reached the back door and he continued on.

"Wait!" she cried. "I thought you meant— Aren't we going to look at the house?"

"My lord, please!" Dansky shouted behind them.

"Pete, what are you up to?" Maisie called, huffing as she tried to keep up.

Pete stopped and looked back at the three people behind him and the princess. "I'm showing Beth around. And we don't need chaperons. Do we, darlin'?''

Watching her struggle for a response, he admitted she was a beauty. Maybe that was the reason he wanted to kiss her again. But he'd kissed other beautiful women.

"I...I think my escorts would like to see the...the house," she said.

He was surprised by her hesitant answer. She'd been quite imperious to everyone the last time he'd met her. If she was going to be agreeable, he'd have to turn up the heat.

Leaning closer, only an inch or two from her luscious lips, he whispered, "But I want to show you around without those clowns following us. I want to be alone with you."

She blinked rapidly, her eyes widening in surprise. Then she turned her head to look at the two men behind her.

Their astounded expressions offered no assistance. Reverting to his earlier opinion of her, she lifted her chin and stared down her royal nose. "These gentlemen need to see the house so they can determine its safety."

"Good," Pete agreed pleasantly, knowing he had her trapped now. "Because I'm showing you the ranch while they look at the house. Maisie? Take these gentlemen on a tour of the house."

Before anyone could respond, he pulled Princess Elsbeth out onto the porch. Then he stepped down and turned, grabbing her by her small waist and swinging her down beside him.

"My shoes!" she shrieked.

With good reason. She was wearing stiletto heels that promptly sank into the dirt, anchoring her. She grabbed his arm as his forward movement almost made her fall.

He ran his gaze down her legs and wondered what his next move should be. Damn, she had great legs! "Take 'em off."

"I'd ruin my stockings! This is ridiculous. If you insist on taking me outdoors, at least let me change my attire."

"Since you knew you were coming to a ranch, why did you dress like that, anyway?"

She lifted that stubborn little chin again. "Because I must maintain my image."

"Well, hell, darlin', I wouldn't want my cowboys to miss seeing you in all your glory." Without any further explanation, he swung her up against his chest.

She came right out of her heels, shrieking and clutching his neck. "Wait! Stop! My shoes!"

"Princess, you worry more about your footwear than anyone I know." As he strode toward the horse barn, he suddenly realized he was enjoying his charade more than he'd expected.

LIZ CLUTCHED his strong neck and stared at his face as he moved. It showed not a speck of strain, as if she weighed next to nothing. But she didn't. After all, she was five foot six without those torturous shoes.

And what did this wild man have in mind? Liz had a feeling she wasn't going to like it, whatever it was.

She ignored the thought of another kiss and the excitement it brought.

In spite of herself, her breathing sped up.

A noise behind her had her looking over his shoulder to discover Dansky and Petrocelli hurrying after her. Thank God they hadn't abandoned her.

She almost laughed at the picture they made. Dansky, though not as tall as the cowboy, still towered over Petrocelli. But both of them were puffing like steam engines. She suspected neither of them could've carried her more than two feet.

At least Petrocelli had discovered her shoes. He clutched them one in each hand as he struggled to catch up with Lord Peter.

The cowboy must've heard them, too.

"Go back to the house!" he ordered over his shoulder, never stopping.

"My lord!" Dansky shouted, but he didn't say anything else. Liz suspected it was because he didn't have the breath.

She would've found the procession they made humorous, Maisie now having joined in the pursuit, if she didn't suspect she was in the clutches of a madman. Or a sex maniac.

"My lord, I really don't think—"

"Call me Pete, darlin'. We don't need to stand on formalities, do we?" He didn't slow down.

"Um, aren't you getting tired? I'm too heavy to—"

"You're just right for what I have in mind." That evil grin he'd used earlier had returned to his face.

Which should've scared her to death. But once

again there was a gleam in his eyes that said he was enjoying himself.

She had a cousin who'd teased her most of her childhood back in Kansas with just such a gleam in his eyes. So while she should've been scared of this man, she wasn't. She was just scared of what he was going to do.

They reached a large barn and he kicked the half-open door farther open with his boot and went inside. The light was dim, and Liz was filled with a sense of homecoming she hadn't felt in five years, the aroma of hay and animals filling her nostrils. It brought back memories of accompanying her father on his rounds.

Her sentimental feelings were erased at once as Pete began to ease her down his body. The sensations that filled her were anything but calm. Her earlier impression of his muscles was confirmed as she seemed to rub against every hard ounce of him. And wanted to do it again.

Before she could draw breath to protest—and she was going to protest, wasn't she?—he shocked her again by tossing her onto a pile of hay. Then he launched his big muscled frame on top of her and locked his lips on hers. Again.

"MY LORD!" Dansky's words were accompanied by a panting that undermined any authority he wanted to convey.

"Go away," Pete muttered, his gaze never leaving the princess's beautiful face. If her expression was anything to go by, she'd enjoyed the kiss as much as he had.

Enjoyment hadn't been his intent. In fact, he'd thought she'd come up shrieking about being treated so roughly, getting so dirty. *He* knew the hay was clean because he'd tossed it himself. But *she* didn't know that.

"My lord," Dansky repeated, but this time he seemed to have recovered slightly from their race to the barn. "Princess Elsbeth should not be treated—"

"Like a fiancée?" Pete asked, reluctantly loosening his hold of her and rearing up on one elbow to face her companions. "I thought that's what she wanted to be, my fiancée."

Petrocelli decided to chime in. "Princess Elsbeth is not used to such rough handling, my lord. I'm sure you understand."

Pete looked down at the woman still lying beneath him. "Is that right, darlin'? I'm being too rough?"

As if his words had awakened her, she punched his chest and squirmed beneath him, trying to escape. "I'm not used to such treatment. And you are definitely moving too quickly. We haven't— I'm not—"

"Neither you nor your father thought it was too soon to become engaged, Princess," he drawled, irritated by the touch of compassion he felt. "You can't have everything your way," he added as he got to his feet. He had to separate his body from hers before her movement made his response too obvious.

She stood up, too, carefully dusting the hay from her suit, then lifted that chin again—and he immediately fantasized trailing kisses down to her slender neck—and below.

"I don't see why not. I'm a princess."

"But you're in America, where there are no princesses," he reminded her.

Her delicate brows arched and she faced him fully for the first time since they'd entered the barn. "But there are gentlemen, aren't there?"

He grinned. "Sure there are…somewhere. But not here."

"Pete!" Maisie protested, pushing forward. "Your grandpa would have a fit if he could hear you."

"Would he?" Pete asked, not willing to explain his plan to anyone.

"My lord, even—" Dansky began.

Pete cut him off. "I'm tired of all this formality. My name is Pete. Don't use that title again. It has no place here."

"But, my lord—" Dansky came to an abrupt halt when Pete glared at him. "Pete, Princess Elsbeth has had an arduous journey. I'm sure she would like to retire to her quarters for a rest."

"A rest?" Pete chuckled. "On a ranch, no one rests until the sun goes down. We work hard."

"But my— Pete," Petrocelli objected, "the princess is not an employee here."

"There are no layabouts on this ranch. If the princess intends to live here, she'll pull on her boots and work like the rest of us." He turned to see how his words affected the delicate, beautiful woman beside him.

She showed no emotion. "Then I'll have to do some shopping, because I have no boots."

Had he misjudged his opponent? he wondered, his eyes narrowing. Her reputation as a party girl was well-known in Europe. She should've handled his touch more easily. After all, he was under no illusions he was dealing with a virgin.

Work, however, should've frightened her to death. Yet she appeared to take it in stride.

"And I suppose you'll need a year or two to find a good pair of boots?"

She met his scornful look without blinking. "Are the stores that far away in Montana?"

Maisie laughed until he turned to look at her. She was supposed to be on his side!

"Have you ever been on a horse before?" He was determined to put this glamorous woman in her place. After all, her silk suit and stiletto heels weren't the garb of a cowgirl.

"Yes, I have." Her chin tipped even higher.

"Western saddle or one of those English pancakes?"

"I don't see what difference—" she began.

"Which tells me how useless you'll be," he growled. *Back down, lady. Hightail it out of here. Run while you can!*

His silent messages didn't seem to reach her. She turned from him and imperiously held out a hand to Petrocelli. Pete hadn't realized the man had retrieved the high heels she'd shed earlier.

Her escort knelt at her feet and slipped the heels on first one slim foot and then the other. When she turned back to Pete, she was several inches taller, the top of her head almost reaching his eyes.

"Perhaps I am not an American cowgirl, Pete,"

she said, using his name for the first time. "But I do not frighten easily."

He'd been afraid of that.

Then she screamed.

LIZ THOUGHT she'd trumped her host's demands with her remark until something furry brushed against her ankle. In the dim shadows she had no idea what kind of animal it was, and she'd let loose a yell.

Pete gave a shout of laughter that made her want to punch him in the gut. Already she could tell the man loved tormenting her.

"Oh? So you're not easily frightened?" He bent down and scooped up a cat, lifting it to her face. "Meet Tabby, our barn cat. Ferocious, isn't she?"

"I was startled," she muttered. To prove her bravery, she took the cat from him and stroked the soft fur.

"No, Your Highness!" Dansky snatched the cat from her hands.

"It's just a cat," she protested.

"But have you forgotten your allergy to cat hair?" He turned to Pete. "The princess loves cats, but she begins to sneeze if she is around them very long."

"But she can ride horses with no problem?" the cowboy asked, clearly skeptical.

"She has not ridden often," Dansky said apologetically.

Great, Liz thought. Obviously they'd neglected to inform her of more than a few things about the woman she was pretending to be. And about the man next to her.

Time to halt the action until she was better informed.

"If you don't mind, I believe I will rest for a while before the evening meal. Tomorrow I promise I will not be so poor a guest."

"But you haven't seen much of anything," Pete said. He reached out as if he intended to prevent her from leaving.

She moved away. She couldn't afford to let Pete tempt her with his touch again. She wasn't sure she could stay in control. "Am I not remaining a week? Must I see everything the first day?"

"'Course you want to rest," Maisie said, unexpectedly coming to her rescue. "I don't know what's gotten into you, Pete, bein' such a poor host. And you clean up before you come to my table," she added, then took Liz's arm and led her to the barn door.

Liz caught one last glimpse of Pete before she exited the barn. Pure exasperation filled his gaze.

"I have your rooms all ready," Maisie informed her as they stepped out into the glorious sunshine. "We won't eat for a couple of hours yet, so you'll have time to unpack and rest."

"Thank you," Liz replied. Out of the corner of her eye she saw Dansky shake his head no. Oh, boy, she'd forgotten that Princess Elsbeth never thanked anyone.

He and Petrocelli had been quick to leave the barn with her. Not that she blamed them. If Pete had been difficult with her, he'd been even less welcoming to her companions.

"Should I help you unpack? We're not used to royalty here."

She smiled at Maisie's worried look. "No, it is not necessary. I can—"

"*We'll* take care of the princess," Dansky interjected.

Maisie turned amazed eyes on the two men. "You will unpack for the princess? Men in Europe must be a lot different than the ones here. I can't hardly get Pete to pick up his underwear off the floor, much less take care of someone else's."

Liz fought to hide her amusement. Somehow she didn't think Pete would want his housekeeper sharing such secrets. But she could just picture— Oops, better not. Any thought of the strong muscular cowboy in his natural state wasn't a good idea.

"My maid fell ill and was unable to accompany me, so I must make do with these gentlemen's assistance," she assured the housekeeper. After all, she had to keep up her part.

"Maybe they could teach Pete a thing or two," Maisie suggested. The look in her blue eyes reminded Liz of the gleam she'd seen in Pete's earlier.

Dansky's warning stare intruded on the smile she exchanged with Maisie, telling her she was being too friendly. She shrugged but said nothing else.

Maisie led her into the house, up the stairs and through the first door on the right. "This here's our best room. It's across the hall from Pete's," she said, gesturing to the closed door on the left.

"I figured the other two would want to be close to you, so their rooms are the next two," she added.

Liz stared at the beautiful room. A king-size bed covered in a colorful quilt dominated the decor. Numerous pillows in the red and blue of the quilt were piled at the head of it. A small sofa faced the huge fireplace at the other end of the room, flanked by easy chairs and lamps. Bookshelves filled the corners, and large windows looked out on the ranchland.

"It's gorgeous, Maisie," she murmured. The older woman smiled back at her, clearly pleased by her response.

"Your bathroom is through that door. The closet is over here. If you need anything, you just let me know."

"Her Highness will relay any requests through us," Dansky corrected in his haughtiest voice, then ushered Maisie out the door and closed it solidly behind her.

"MAISIE, WHAT THE HELL were you doing?" Pete demanded a few minutes later. He'd come back into the house and discovered his housekeeper busy in the kitchen.

"What do you mean?" she asked, barely glancing up from the apples she was peeling.

"I mean helping that woman escape my clutches, and you know it."

"Your grandpa wouldn't want you to treat anyone that way, much less your wife-to-be."

"That's the point, Maisie. I don't want her to be my wife."

"Why not?"

He was puzzled by Maisie's look, one of stubborn

resistance. What had gotten into her? She'd always been his biggest supporter. "Why would you ask that, Maisie? You don't want some highfalutin princess running around here giving you orders, do you?"

Instead of answering his question, she muttered, "I like her."

He moved to her side so he could get a clearer look at her face. "What?"

"I like her. She's…she's nice."

"Don't let her fool you. She's a spoiled, pampered woman who will never pull her own weight around here." He was sure of that, at least.

"But she might have babies."

Pete felt as if the air had been knocked out of him. "Babies?" he gasped.

"Your grandpa hoped you'd marry and have a son to inherit the ranch."

"Then he shouldn't have left the ranch to my mother. She's going to sell it out from under me."

"No, she won't. Mary Margaret may have the bit between her teeth, but she wouldn't do that."

Pete wished he could be as sure as Maisie. But his mother had changed a lot since she'd simply been Mary Margaret. Now she was the dowager Duchess of Hereford. And nothing in America, even her birthright, was as important as her life in England.

"Even if I was going to have…have babies, I wouldn't want a princess for their mother. I need a good American girl—like you," he said, hoping the flattery would bring Maisie back to his side.

She turned to stare at him, reminding him of the times she'd caught him with his hand in the cookie jar or slipping in late after his grandfather had gone to bed. "I like her," she insisted, implacable. "Wouldn't hurt you to please your mother and yourself."

"And how do you think marrying this woman would please me?" he growled.

"You seemed happy enough in the barn with her plastered against you. She's a beautiful woman, after all." Maisie shot him a look that dared him to deny her words.

He couldn't. He couldn't say she wasn't beautiful. And he couldn't say he'd been unhappy when he'd held her in his arms. "There are beautiful American women."

"'Course there are. But you don't seem too interested in them. You're not gettin' any younger, you know."

"I'm thirty-two, Maisie, not eighty-two."

"A good thing, too. You need energy to chase after young'uns."

"Maisie, this conversation is not about babies!"

Maisie sniffed and returned to the apples. "Well, it should be."

With a frustrated growl Pete left the kitchen and headed for the stairs and the shower. Even he was tired of smelling himself, and Maisie wasn't in a reasonable mood. He didn't intend to stand around arguing about having babies.

Even if the idea of making them was…intriguing.

Chapter Three

"I think you neglected to inform me of a few things,"
Liz said the moment her escort shut the bedroom
door.

"Lord Peter's manner is not... It has changed. We
were not aware he would be this difficult," Dansky
said, his apologetic respectful attitude gone now.

Liz's eyebrows soared. "Difficult? I think that's an
understatement. Though not quite as startling as the
revelation that the man is my fiancé. Don't you think
you should've mentioned that fact?"

She remembered the first interview with the two
men. She'd seen them exchange silent looks, just as
they were doing now. Her instincts had warned her,
but the lure of the money to help her mother had
caused her to ignore them.

"Your Highness, we truly did not think the engagement would be a concern," Petrocelli finally
said.

She stared at the little man, unable to believe his
words. "You didn't think... Why ever not? The man
thinks I'm going to marry him!"

"Not you," Dansky said. "The princess."

"Oh, thanks for that clarification! But I'm the one he was kissing in the barn." She willed her cheeks to remain pale, but even the thought of their embrace was enough to warm her all over.

"Yes, and you must not allow such intimacies in the future," Dansky said sternly.

Liz practically sputtered. "Do you think the kiss was my idea?" Really! How could the man imply she had initiated it? She drew a deep breath. True, she hadn't exactly fought Pete, but...but she was only human.

"Why am I here?" she asked abruptly.

"We explained," Petrocelli said. "Princess Elsbeth needed a decoy so she wouldn't be followed by the press."

Liz shook her head. "She doesn't need a decoy to come here. There's no press. Only a fiancé who expects more than I'm prepared to offer. Now come clean."

They didn't like her giving orders. The affront on Dansky's face would've been laughable if she hadn't needed an explanation. Petrocelli showed a slight sign of a conscience.

"Your Highness, the situation is difficult to explain...and you're being well paid."

Her cheeks flushed at the reminder. Wasn't that always how the con men got their victims—by appealing to their greed? She admitted it. But her mother needed her help. And Liz's five years in Hollywood hadn't exactly brought riches.

But this job description hadn't included a fiancé.

Even as anxious as she was to help her mother, she wouldn't have agreed to that.

"Look, you didn't tell me Lord Peter would be... You said this was a formal visit, nothing else. I'd stay here for a week, so the press wouldn't hound the real princess, and then the princess, the real princess, would return to her country."

"Nothing has changed," Dansky told her stiffly.

"Oh, yeah? That kiss wasn't formal!" she snapped, her cheeks turning an even brighter red.

"Which one?" Dansky asked dryly.

Not about to be intimidated, she returned, "Either one!"

"Shh!" Petrocelli warned. "We did not expect the man to become...to insist on such intimacy."

"He's her fiancé and you didn't expect him to do more than shake hands? That's ridiculous."

Dansky clearly didn't appreciate her words. "In Europe marriages of convenience are arranged frequently without any...any physical relationship."

"Well, welcome to America."

Again Petrocelli tried to soothe her. "I'm sure Lord Peter will be reasonable when we explain your aversion to intimacy before the wedding. They do still have virgins in America, don't they?"

"The princess is a virgin?"

Now the men's faces flooded with color. Liz watched them speculatively, wondering how Petrocelli would handle this question.

"I cannot answer that question. Her experience is not any of our business. But Lord Peter will accept our explanation."

Maybe. But he might have a big surprise on his wedding night if these two were lying.

"You still haven't explained why the princess isn't here. I thought I was coming to a dude ranch or...or a house party. If this man is her fiancé, why isn't she here?"

"The princess is...willful," Dansky finally said, as if he'd revealed a terrible thing. "She wanted a week's freedom, but her father, the king, refused. He doesn't know that...that she is in hiding."

Liz stared at the two men. "He doesn't know?"

Petrocelli shook his head sadly.

"Is she going to go through with the wedding?"

"She has no choice. Her country's economy is dependent on this union."

Liz felt as if she'd stumbled into a beehive. How could a simple job...? But she should've known better. Georgia's jobs never paid a hundred thousand.

"I can't do this," she suddenly announced. "You'll have to find someone else."

"That's impossible. You've already been introduced as the princess. You look just like her. We couldn't find anyone else now," Dansky insisted, glowering at her.

"And you've taken our money," Petrocelli reminded her.

She had. And immediately forwarded it to her mother so she could pay off debts. With the news that she, Liz, would be returning home after this week.

"I'll pay you back. I can't do this!" Memories of the cowboy who'd swept her into his arms assured her she couldn't.

"We must insist. Our country's future is at stake," Dansky said. "If the royal family falls, so will our country."

"The tourist business that would come from a royal wedding will do wonders for our economy," Petrocelli said. When she didn't respond, he added softly, going to the heart of the matter, "One of us will remain with you at all times. The cowboy will not be able to do anything to you."

Liz sank her teeth into her bottom lip. Talk about a good news/bad news scenario. The man could kiss the daylights out of her, start a fire in her that threatened to consume her, make her want more than she'd ever wanted from a man. But he wouldn't. Mutt and Jeff wouldn't allow it.

"I'm not sure he'll be that easy to control."

In fact, everything she'd seen so far had pointed to a man determined to get his own way.

"You must not encourage him," Dansky urged.

She slapped her hands on her hips in anger. "I beg your pardon?" He said nothing and she asked, "Do you think I encouraged him to kiss me, to shanghai me to the barn? I don't think so."

"You did not protest!" Dansky returned.

"I didn't know if I was supposed to. If you'd told me what was going on, I might've had some idea." She glared back at him.

Before he could respond, her door swung open and the center of her difficulties leaned against the doorjamb, his arms crossed over his broad chest.

"Darlin', if you're going to entertain in your bedroom, I insist the only man allowed in is me."

Liz stared at Pete, frantically wondering how much he'd overheard, distracted by his suggestive words. "I...I... They are to unpack for me."

"We are here to protect and serve the princess, sir," Dansky said stiffly.

Since Pete didn't erupt into anger, calling them all liars, Liz assumed he hadn't heard anything damaging. Just as she began to relax, however, he had another suggestion.

"Well, if they're going to do all the grunt work, darlin', you and I can have some time alone." He straightened from his sexy slouch and held out his hand.

"No!" she protested, self-defense prompting her, "I have to supervise."

"Darlin', you got to learn to delegate. They'll manage without you." He came closer and she backed up until her legs were resting against the bed.

Petrocelli stepped between them. "The princess will lie down while we work, thereby supervising us and resting at the same time. She will look forward to seeing you at dinner, Pete."

Pete stood with both hands on his hips, balanced on the balls of his feet, as if ready to launch himself at an enemy. Liz held her breath. He was a formidable foe.

After what seemed like eons, he relaxed and grinned wryly at Petrocelli. "You seem awful worried about protecting Beth from me. I don't intend to hurt her."

"Of course not, my lord—I mean, Pete. But it has been a long day for the princess. After we have put away her belongings, I would be pleased to assist you as your valet,'' he added, his gaze traveling up and down Pete's body.

Liz almost laughed out loud. Pete looked as outraged as a five-year-old boy expected to dress in a tux.

''I can manage on my own!'' he snapped, then spun on his heel and left.

When the door slammed shut behind him, she let out her pent-up breath and smiled at the short man.

''Nice job, Petrocelli. A great rout.''

The man bowed and smiled in return. ''I think he will not bother you until you emerge for dinner.''

She didn't think so, either. And that was a good thing, in spite of her being drawn to the cowboy. He might be handsome, but if he found out she wasn't the real thing, all hell would break loose.

''YOU WANT TO WHAT?'' Maisie asked, staring at him as if he'd lost his head.

''It's no big deal, Maisie. Just cook a few more steaks. You've got a couple of hours to get ready. I'll even get Joseph to come help you.''

''That good-for-nothing in my kitchen? I don't think so. The men always eat in the bunkhouse kitchen. Why are they comin' here tonight?''

Pete turned his back on Maisie's penetrating gaze. ''So Beth can meet all of them. They're anxious to see her, to find out if anything is going to be changed. I figure life will go more smoothly if we get that first meeting out of the way.'' He was proud of himself.

His rationale sounded logical, even if it wasn't the truth.

"Meetin' 'em and eatin' with 'em ain't the same. Some of those boys ain't got no manners. She'll be disgusted."

That was what he hoped. Pete hadn't made much progress with sending the princess running. With those two gorillas guarding her every step, he wasn't sure how effective his plan would be. He was counting on his men to show her she wasn't in sophisticated society anymore.

"They're good men, Maisie," he finally said.

"'Course they are. That don't make them graceful."

"She needs to discover what life here is like."

"*You* don't eat with 'em every day. Why should she?"

Maisie's arguments were valid, he had to admit, but he wasn't going to give in. "Just do what I say."

She stared at him, trying to read into his soul. She'd always been a pro at that, but Pete hoped she failed tonight.

"We'll have to eat in the dining room. This here table isn't big enough."

He almost groaned when he thought about the Oriental carpet his grandfather had brought back from a trip to Turkey. "Uh, maybe we should roll up the rug and put it away, then."

"If you want. And we'll have to use the crystal and china of course."

"No! No, let's use the regular dishes. I know you have enough of them." As he finished, he turned to his housekeeper and caught a look in her eyes. She'd been testing him. "Maisie, you rat. You know I don't want—"

"Yeah, I know. Go roll up the rug."

THE AFTERNOON had been interesting, Liz thought, but she expected the evening to be more so. Watching two men put away a wardrobe she'd never worn while she lay stretched out on the big bed was a new experience. Wearing the outfit they had selected was different, too. She'd protested its formality, but Petrocelli had assured her the princess must always be appropriately dressed.

So she came down the stairs in green silk, the skirt swirling about her legs, encased in stockings that led to more high heels. She was beginning to think the real princess had a shoe fetish. Or maybe it was Dansky.

That thought had her smiling until she encountered the gaze of her fiancé.

"You're happy?" he asked, with that belligerent hands-on-hips stance he'd shown earlier.

"Of course. You have a lovely home."

"I'm thinking of tearing it down."

Such a statement might've shocked her if she hadn't read frustration in his gaze. "Oh?"

"Takes too much money to maintain." Without waiting for a response, he turned and charged into the kitchen.

Petrocelli cleared his throat. "Perhaps we should retire to the lounge, Your Highness. I'm sure our host will serve drinks there."

Dansky didn't hide his disgust. "I hope these heathens practice such common courtesies. I, for one, am in need of spirits."

With a shrug Liz headed in the direction of the parlor. Before she could take more than a couple of steps, Maisie came through the door where Pete had disappeared.

"Your Highness," she said hurriedly, and sketched a brief curtsy. "I didn't know you was down yet."

"Please, Maisie, there's no need to be formal."

Maisie smiled at her even as Liz heard mutterings from her companions.

"Good. Pete has invited all the boys to meet you this evening. I hope you don't mind."

"The boys?"

"His employees and all."

"Oh. No, of course I do not mind. Shall we…um, where shall we go?"

"This way. To the dining room. The kitchen table is too small." She bustled past the trio and led the way toward the front of the house. "Most of 'em's already there."

Maisie swung a door open and Liz saw, over her shoulder, a large well-proportioned room filled with cowboys. Pete was there, so obviously there was a connecting door to the kitchen. He was pouring drinks for his guests at an antique buffet that lined one wall.

"Ah," Dansky muttered. He took a step toward Pete and then halted, turning to Liz.

It was the first time she'd seen Dansky forget himself.

"Your Highness, what would you like to drink?"

"Nothing, thank you."

Both men appeared shocked by her response. Petrocelli leaned closer. "You always ask for white wine."

"But I don't care for any."

"Dansky will bring you some," Petrocelli murmured.

When Liz turned to argue with him, she saw Maisie staring at them, making an argument impossible. With regal hauteur, she nodded. And only prayed she wouldn't be required to drink it. When she drank wine, she broke out in large red splotches. Not exactly a regal attribute.

The room suddenly quieted, as if its occupants had just noticed her entrance. She smiled at the awkward expressions on the men's faces, hoping her friendliness would ease the situation.

One sturdy cowboy, old enough to be her grandfather and clutching a beer bottle, stepped forward. "Welcome, Princess."

Liz could smell a combination of man and animal sweat and a few other pungent odors associated with a hardworking cowboy. Even as she prepared to thank him, Petrocelli moved in front of her and murmured, "The princess should be addressed as Your Highness."

A harsh voice cut in. "We don't stand on formality here," Pete said.

"But, my lord—" Dansky began.

"Pete!" Lord Peter said again, glaring at the man.

"Pete," Dansky muttered, then continued with his

protest. "The princess isn't to be treated like a commoner."

"Why not? We're all the same here."

Dansky opened his mouth to add further argument, but Liz forestalled him. Stepping forward, she offered her hand to the cowboy who'd spoken.

"Why don't you call me Beth, as Pete does?"

The man wiped his right hand on his jeans and then took hers. The skin was rough and calloused, but Liz had no problem with the evidence of hard work. "And your name is?"

"Harvey, ma'am. Harvey Cranton."

Behind her, Liz heard a rumble of footsteps and turned to discover the other cowboys crowding forward to be introduced. She asked Harvey to present her, and one by one they shook her hand, after carefully wiping theirs on their jeans.

When the last man had been introduced, she turned back to Harvey. "Could you perhaps show me where I am to sit?" She placed one well-manicured hand on his arm and smiled at him.

His chest swelled with pride as he said, "Yes, ma'am, Beth, I reckon I could. Since you'll be the lady of the house, you'll sit down here." He led her around the table to its foot and pulled back her chair for her as gallantly as any titled gentleman.

"Thank you so much, Harvey. Will you join me?" she asked, patting the place to her right.

He acted as if she'd offered him a huge prize as he took the chair next to her. Suddenly there was a mad scramble as the rest of the men, nine in all, though it seemed like more, joined them at the table.

Only Petrocelli, Maisie, Dansky and Pete had not taken their places. Liz met Pete's gaze, surprised by the anger she saw there. Didn't he want her to get along with his employees?

Dansky didn't look much happier. He turned back to Pete, who was still taking drink orders, to make his requests.

"White wine?" Pete roared. He turned to Liz again. "Sorry, Beth, but our tastes don't run to such delicacies. Jack Daniel's, maybe, but not white wine."

"That's all right. I really don't need any wine tonight." *Or ever.* Thank goodness he didn't have wine. She'd have to speak to her keepers about her allergy.

"But your grandpa always kept lots of wine," Harvey called out, puzzlement in his voice. "Have you drunk it all, boy?"

Pete tried to ignore Harvey's question. When the cowboy would've persisted, Liz placed a hand on his arm, distracting him.

"I really don't want anything, Harvey." She smiled at the eager faces and waited for the meal to be served.

DAMN! HIS PLAN wasn't working. He'd expected the roughness of his men, all good-hearted but not much trained in the social graces, to offend the princess. After all, she was a jet-setter, not used to anything but the best.

Instead, she had them completely charmed.

"I don't remember the princess being so...so agreeable," he muttered to Dansky.

The man seemed to choke on the drink he'd handed him before clearing his throat and saying, "The princess is always polite. And she's making a special effort to fit in to her new home."

Great. Just what he wanted.

"Well, sit down, boys, and I'll start bringing in the food," Maisie ordered.

"May I..." the princess began.

Pete held his breath. He'd know something was wrong if the woman offered to help with such lowly duties. He stared at her, waiting for her to finish.

With a barely perceptible pause she added, "...offer the services of Petrocelli and Dansky? They will be pleased to assist you, Maisie."

Pete smiled grimly. That was the princess he expected. The one who ordered her servants around.

However, the princess's offer seemed to have inspired his men, much to his surprise. Several of them jumped to their feet, smiling in Beth's direction. "We'll be glad to help, too."

Maisie accepted all offers and led the men from the dining room, leaving Pete to stare after them. He'd never seen his men act like...like well-trained lap dogs. He turned around to glare at Beth. She was changing everything. Maybe she was a witch and had cast a spell on them all.

Harvey, the biggest complainer he'd ever met, was blushing to beat the band and smiling at her. Larry was batting his eyes like a sixteen-year-old girl. And across the table Martin looked as if he was drooling.

Beth was the center of attention. In fact, Pete

could've stood on his head and no one would've noticed.

Well, she wasn't going to ignore him!

Moving to stand beside her, he put his hand on her shoulder, feeling creamy skin that begged for his touch. "Beth, have you met everyone?"

"Yes, thank you. Harvey was kind enough to make the introductions." She smiled at the old cowboy, which for some inexplicable reason made Pete's blood boil.

"Good." Before he could think of something else to say to draw her attention, the kitchen door opened to a procession of helpers, each carrying a large platter.

Maisie, concerned with ordering her troops, still had time to tell Pete to sit down.

He marched to his end of the table with all the righteousness of a Christian martyr. Princess Elsbeth wasn't playing fair. She looked too good to be ignored, but it was her manner, her...sweetness that was capturing his cowboys' hearts. He hadn't counted on that.

After pausing for him to say grace, conversation erupted around the table, another surprise. Most often, cowboys stuffed themselves and then headed back to the barn to do more chores or turned on the television for some amusement. They didn't mess with dinner-table conversations.

He knew the reason. Beth was asking questions about their lives and listening as if she cared. Sneaky behavior on her part.

Maisie was seated on his right, but Petrocelli and

Dansky had taken the first two chairs on his left. He turned to them.

"She said she doesn't have any boots."

The two men exchanged looks. Then Petrocelli spoke. "No, Pete, she does not. That is, she has a pair of fashionable boots, but they would not be suitable for riding."

"Then we'll go get some first thing tomorrow morning. After all, she should become used to the saddle." Since nothing else had worked, he intended to get physical.

Which reminded him of the two kisses they'd exchanged. That kind of physical meant pleasure—unforgettable pleasure, he thought with a sigh. Pleasure he'd like to repeat as soon as possible.

"You okay, Pete?" Maisie asked, shaking him from his thoughts.

Damn! He didn't need to be concentrating on touching the woman, though he remembered how silky her skin had felt beneath his fingers. But she didn't fit into his plans for the future. Only his beloved ranch was in his plans. And he'd better remember that.

"I'm fine," he said. "Good steak, Maisie."

"Your cuisine is excellent, Miss Maisie," Petrocelli added.

To Pete's disgust Maisie blushed. "Thank you, Mr. Petrocelli." After a pause she said, "If you'll give me a list of the princess's preferred food, I'll—"

"She'll eat what we eat!" Pete snapped, his voice hard. He had to fight to keep it that way.

"Pete! She's our guest. I can—"

"If she's going to live here, she'll have to adjust," he muttered. His gaze traveled the length of the table to the beautiful woman.

Oh, yeah. If she stayed, there'd be some major adjusting taking place. The only problem was, he was afraid he'd be the one making the changes. Nope! Wasn't going to happen.

"I'm sure anything you prepare will be acceptable to the princess," Petrocelli said quietly, pleasing Maisie, Pete could tell, even if it irritated him.

Maisie beamed at him. "What time does she get up?"

"Same time as the rest of us!"

"Pete!" Maisie protested.

"I'm not having some pampered guest upsetting everything around here, Maisie. We get up with the sun," he informed Petrocelli, "and that's when the princess will get up, too." He sneaked a look at Beth at the other end of the table, oblivious to his strictures.

Dansky intervened. "The princess is not used to such early rising, my lord. She will not be able to do so."

"Then she'd better find somewhere else to live," Pete replied. He really made an effort to keep his voice calm, but he thought he might've scored a knockout blow.

Again Beth's cohorts looked at each other. Petrocelli leaned toward Pete. "What time does the sun rise here?"

He hadn't expected that question. "I'm up at six. Maisie puts breakfast on the table at six-thirty. I'm not having her wear herself out by serving breakfast all morning long. She has other things to do.''

"Pete?'' Beth called from the other end of the table.

His head snapped up and he stared at her. "What?''

The grouchiness of that one word had his entire family of cowboys staring as if he'd just handed her an insult.

"I am sorry if I interrupted you. But Harvey has offered to take me riding tomorrow. Do you have a mount that I might use?''

Pete sat there, frustration mounting. How could he answer? He wanted to say she'd have to ride all day long, like his cowboys, but he knew he'd be branded an evil man if he said such a thing in front of them. Beth had already convinced them she was an angel.

And they all knew there were plenty of horses on the ranch guests could use. So he had no choice but to agree to her request.

"Yeah, there's a horse. But you'll need boots and jeans.'' That wasn't an unreasonable request. But as he pictured her in tight jeans, he felt his mouth go dry. Maybe it was a request he shouldn't have made.

"Is there a store nearby where I can purchase such items?''

"I'll be glad to take you,'' Harvey immediately offered.

Pete was going to have to have a talk with Harvey. Of all the men on his staff, he'd thought Harvey would support him. "I thought you were supposed to move that herd in the north pasture tomorrow,'' he reminded him.

"Well, shoot, boss, I can—"

He stopped when Beth touched his arm again. Damn it, she was always touching Harvey. He hadn't noticed her trying to touch *him*.

"It's all right, Harvey. I don't want to interrupt your work. Dansky and Petrocelli will arrange everything."

Pete should've been pleased she didn't want to interfere with the running of his ranch. He should've been happy she could take care of herself. Most of all, he should've been relieved he wouldn't have to spend any time with her.

But he wasn't.

"If anyone takes you shopping around here, it'll be me," he said, continuing to glare at the woman who was making his life a misery.

"Why, thank you, Pete. That's most kind of you." She gave him a cheerful smile and turned her attention back to her meal.

Pete, however, had no interest in his own half-eaten steak. He was pretty sure he'd just made a big mistake.

Chapter Four

"Darling boy, did she arrive?"

Pete groaned and leaned back against the pillow, cradling the phone against his ear.

"Mother, it's five in the morning."

"I thought you cowboy types always got up early, dearest. The last time you visited, the peacocks were still sleeping when you prowled the house."

Because he'd been restless, eager to return to America. Eager to get out from under his mother's eye. He cleared his throat. "Not quite this early, Mother. Why are you calling?"

"To see if Princess Elsbeth arrived. She's beautiful, isn't she?"

"Yes, she arrived, and yes, she's...attractive." So attractive he'd had trouble getting to sleep last night.

"Are you on your best behavior?"

"I'm not a little boy, Mother."

Silence prevailed and he hoped he'd satisfied her. But he had a sinking feeling he hadn't.

Abruptly she said, "I'm flying over."

"What?" He practically leaped upright in his bed.

"What did you say?" That was all he needed. His mother *and* the princess. He frantically sought reasons to keep her in England. "Robert needs you, Mother."

"Nonsense. You know your brother would enjoy a few days' peace." She gave a big sigh. "Though I only try to help both my children, neither of you seems to appreciate my efforts."

The lonely tones made him feel like a selfish son, but he steeled himself to ignore those feelings. The dowager duchess was an actress par excellence.

"Mother, really, there's no need. I assure you the princess is being well taken care of. She has two escorts who are waiting on her hand and foot."

"Then how do the two of you spend time alone?"

He couldn't think of an answer. While his plan had called for him to get Beth alone and scare her away, he'd discovered a problem. If and when he got her alone, he wanted to kiss her.

Not a good idea.

"That settles it. I'm coming. Ta-ta."

Before he could say anything else, the phone went dead. Even if he called her back at once, he knew he wouldn't be able to stop her from flying all the way from England to ensure that his love life suited her.

What a way to start his day.

LIZ PEEKED at the stern man behind the wheel of the truck. He looked tired. For all his demands she be at the breakfast table at six-thirty sharp, he had been the one to come in late. But he'd come from the barn, not his bedroom, indicating he'd already been at work.

Now he was taking her to buy jeans and boots, and she felt guilty adding to his chores.

"My mother is coming," he said abruptly, his face grim.

"Oh?" What was she supposed to say? Did she know his mother? She cast a frantic look at her escorts, riding in the small back seat of the truck cab.

"Her Highness will enjoy visiting with the dowager duchess again," Petrocelli said smoothly, nodding to Liz, she supposed, in encouragement.

Knowing she, not Liz but the real princess, had met Pete's mother before only made matters worse. Liz didn't know how or when.

"Yeah, right." Pete didn't sound like he believed Petrocelli's words.

"Do you not want your mother to visit?" she asked, curious about his tone.

He gave her a burning stare that seared her. Wrong question apparently.

She tried again. "Does she visit often?"

"No."

Well, that conversational gambit hadn't worked. She shrugged and turned her attention to the scenery, breathtaking by anyone's standards. After having grown up in Kansas, she loved the grandeur of the mountains. In winter, coated in snow, the mountains must look incredible.

"Have you made a list?" the man beside her growled.

"A list?"

"A shopping list. I don't have all day. There's work to be done back at the ranch."

He acted as if she'd intentionally set out to wreck his day. With a sweetness designed to irritate him, she said, "I'm so sorry to take up your time. You should've stayed at the ranch. Dansky and Petrocelli, or Harvey, could've brought me shopping."

His fingers tightened on the wheel until his knuckles were almost white, showing her she'd scored against his grouchiness. They were such nice hands, too. Too bad they showed so much anger. When he'd stroked her back, she'd— No! She wasn't going to think about that embrace in the barn.

"I said I'd bring you shopping and I have. I just wanted to know if you had a list."

"No. I thought I'd get some jeans and boots, maybe a couple of shirts. Will I need anything else?"

"Some good socks, a hat." He continued to stare at the road in front of him, but the corners of his mouth twitched before he added, "And maybe a bottle of linament."

The meanie was looking forward to her discomfort. Wasn't he going to be surprised when he discovered her riding ability! She'd ridden all her life. In Los Angeles her riding had been limited by her finances, but when she could afford it, she'd gone to a local stable. "Oh, really? You think—"

"Her Highness will not ride very much," Dansky intruded, his voice sharp.

She turned to look at him and saw the warning in his eyes. Darn! She'd been looking forward to spending time in the saddle.

"If she's going to live on the ranch, she'll ride,"

was Pete's stubborn response. The finality in his tone ended that discussion.

Determined not to let him have the last word, she said in dulcet tones, "But I am only *visiting* this week."

"My grandfather always said, 'Begin as you mean to go on,'" he said, still refusing to look at her.

"Her Highness will not be able to remain at the ranch for long periods of time, Pete. She has many duties in her homeland she cannot escape. You will also be expected to accompany her on these trips," Petrocelli said.

"Nope."

Liz wondered if the two escorts were as stunned as she. "You mean you have no intention of fulfilling your duties as my husband?"

"The only duty as your husband that I intend to fulfill will take place in the first bed we come to. Other than that, it's your role as wife to meet *my* needs, not your country's. You'll be American after we marry."

She stiffened, her cheeks flaming at his reference to a bed. "I believe you are what American women call a chauvinist pig!"

"Yeah."

"You do not argue?"

"Nope. And if you don't like it, hightail it back to Cargenia." They had reached town while they talked, and now he pulled into a parking space in front of a small store.

Without a word, he opened the truck door and got

out, slamming it behind him. Liz stared at him as he entered the store.

"I believe we are to accompany him," Petrocelli said softly.

"*I* believe this marriage is going to be a disaster," she said in return, turning to stare at the two men. "Are you sure we shouldn't just call the whole thing off?"

Dansky looked outraged, but it was Petrocelli who replied. "That is not our decision, Your Highness. Only your father can make that decision."

"My father has control over whether or not I marry someone? That's barbaric!"

"Please, Your Highness—" Dansky began.

"You need to inform him that Lord Peter is not cooperating. He will agree that the marriage is best forgotten and we can all get out of here." She ignored the sadness that welled up in her at the thought of leaving. But it was the only sensible thing to do.

"We cannot—"

The door beside Liz opened and she almost fell into the arms of the impossible man under discussion.

"Are you going to shop or aren't you?" he growled.

His face was very close to hers and she had to concentrate to answer. "I thought perhaps you would make the selections for me, since my only role in life is to please you."

He didn't appreciate her sarcasm. But his response took her by surprise. Without a word he encircled her waist with his big hands and lifted her out of the truck. "Come on, before I turn you over my knee and spank you."

"Oh? So you are brutal, as well as self-centered?"

Surprisingly he ignored her taunt. "Don't embarrass me in front of my friends," he muttered as he took her arm and led her into the small store.

Ah, so he did have some vulnerability. But she couldn't hurt him that way. Pasting on a gracious smile, she greeted the shop owner warmly as Pete introduced her, extending her hand. The man, in his fifties, bowed as he clasped her fingers.

"Please, that is not necessary. As Pete will tell you, there are no princesses in America," she said with a chuckle.

"Ma'am, I sure reckon Pete's wrong about that. Welcome to Parsons, Montana, and our store. What can I do for you?"

"I need some riding clothes so I can go out with the cowboys," she said with a smile.

"My wife'll be glad to outfit you. Phyllis?"

From the back of the store, a woman lifted her head and then came toward them. In a few minutes Liz was placed in Phyllis's hands and found herself in a dressing room. After she'd put on jeans, cowboy boots and a plaid shirt, Phyllis suggested she show her outfit to Pete.

She wasn't interested in giving him any choices in her wardrobe, but without causing a stir, what else could she do?

PETE PACED the aisles of the store as he waited for Beth to emerge from the dressing room. What was she saying to Phyllis? He'd been a little rough on her, but what choice did he have? He certainly wasn't going to be a pet husband, led around by the nose. And he couldn't afford to be away from the ranch often. It was a big operation that required a steady hand.

"What do you think?"

He whirled around to stare at the vision before him. She looked like a cowboy's dream. Snug jeans encasing a rounded female form that made his body tighten, plaid shirt with the neck open, a cowboy hat cocked on her head at a becoming angle.

"She looks great, doesn't she?" Phyllis said. "I'd think she was a real American cowgirl if I didn't know better."

"Yeah," Pete muttered.

Disappointment flickered in Beth's eyes. He hadn't intended to hurt her feelings, but, hell, he couldn't say what he really thought, that he'd like to… No, he couldn't say that. "You'll need gloves."

"Why? It's not cold," she said, staring at her hands.

"Because if you don't wear gloves, your hands won't be soft and lily white anymore."

"Hey, you're not gonna put her to work, are you?" the store owner, Abe, teased.

"Why not? On a ranch we don't have room for slackers." Pete ignored the shocked look on Abe's face. He didn't have to explain himself to anyone.

"Do you have any gloves, Phyllis?" Beth asked calmly.

"'Course I do. Come over here, honey."

Pete frowned as the two women walked away. That

was what was different about Beth. When he'd seen her before, she'd never let anyone forget she was a princess. Here, and on the ranch, *she* had been the one to offer informality.

When all her purchases had been gathered at the front of the store, she turned to her two escorts. "You will take care of the charges?"

Pete stepped forward. "Just put it on my bill, Abe."

"No!" Beth protested. "That is not right. My father—"

Pete waved for the two escorts to pick up the sacks and took her arm without replying. "Thanks, Abe."

"Thank you for your help, Phyllis," Beth called over her shoulder.

"Anytime, Beth. You get tired of those cowboys, come to town and we'll have lunch," Phyllis returned.

Pete tightened his hold on Beth's arm, pulling her from the store before she could answer. He wasn't about to let her loose in town on her own. To start with, she'd attract cowboys like flies to dead meat.

"Why did you do that?" she asked, frowning at him.

The desire to kiss away that frown, to haul her into his arms and tell her she wouldn't get tired of him, wouldn't want to come to town without him, was overwhelming. And disturbing. "I'm in a hurry!" he snapped.

"You don't trust your cowboys to work if you're not there?"

"Of course I do! They're good men. Just because

they're not as polished as your European playboys doesn't mean—''

"*I* have not cast aspersions on your cowboys. It's your lack of confidence in their efforts that has—''

"I have complete confidence in them. I just…don't like to be away from the ranch.''

"Are you shy?''

He came to an abrupt halt and turned to stare at her. Shy? She thought he was shy? He'd show her shy. Without warning, he wrapped his arms around her and did what he'd been dying to do since the last time he'd kissed her. Like a starving man, he melded their lips together, holding her blue-jeaned form tightly against his.

"My lord!'' Dansky exclaimed from somewhere in another world, his voice barely penetrating Pete's pleasure.

With Beth's arms around his neck, there was no need to force her against him, and he let his hands roam, prompted by the need to touch her all over.

She met his eagerness with what he'd swear was an appetite as big as his own. Her fingers threaded through his hair and stroked his neck. Her mouth needed no urging to open to his.

"People are staring,'' Petrocelli warned in a horrified voice.

Pete heard the words, but what did he care when he was in heaven? Her breasts were pressed against his chest and he wanted to touch them so badly he ached. When his hand ventured there, however, he felt Beth's shock. A tremble went through her body and he released her lips to stare at her.

A burst of applause and cowboy whoops interrupted the love fest as much as his withdrawal. Beth's eyes were wide with shock.

"Way to go, Pete!" an acquaintance shouted. "Who's the lady?"

"A friend," he returned, his gaze never leaving Beth's face. He wanted to kiss her again, to shut out the world, leaving only his desires and pleasures. But he couldn't. "I think we'd better get out of here," he whispered.

"Come on, Pete, aren't you gonna introduce us?" another man called.

"Not on your life, Spellman. I wouldn't introduce you to my worst enemy, much less a lady. You all need to get a life and stay out of mine!" He tossed a grin over his shoulder as he led Beth back to the truck.

"But yours looks like a lot more fun," the man replied, laughing.

Pete ignored him, putting Beth in the front seat of the truck and rounding it to slide behind the wheel while Petrocelli and Dansky scrambled into the back. With a wave of his hand, he drove off.

Immediately the two men in the back protested his behavior.

"My lord, that was highly inappropriate behavior. Her Highness is not—"

"Oh, shut up," Pete snapped.

"Pete, you must not handle Her Highness in such a manner. She is not used to—"

"I don't need your instructions, Petrocelli."

This time Dansky tried. "But you cannot—"

''Truly, you will offend her father, the king, if—''

''The king can go take a flying leap!'' Pete roared.

''My lord!'' Dansky sounded highly offended.

''Really, Pete, you go too far!'' Petrocelli echoed.

The only person Pete wanted to hear from was not talking. Beth kept her face turned away and stared out the window.

As soon as the truck stopped, Liz got out and ran for the house, headed for the stairs and her bedroom. She desperately needed to be alone.

Too bad.

Three males were hot on her heels. Maisie, hearing the rush of boots, could even be heard asking what was wrong. Liz reached her bedroom before they could catch her, but there was no lock on the door. Even if a closed door would stop her two guards, she knew it would never stop Pete.

She leaned against the door, trying to catch her breath, something that seemed impossible to do when she thought about their embrace on the main street of Parsons. Good heavens! What would those people think of Princess Elsbeth? She, Liz, was supposed to be helping the princess, not ruining her future life.

And how difficult was it going to be for the princess when she discovered the person impersonating her couldn't keep her hands off the princess's future husband? That was the scariest part of all. She knew Petrocelli and Dansky were going to tell her she should've resisted Pete.

And they were right.

But she couldn't. The man was like a magnet, drawing her to him. What was she going to do?

A fist pounded on the door.

"Beth? Open up."

She recognized Pete's voice, followed by calls from the other two. Silently she remained with her back to the door, not answering.

Pete pounded again, but it was Maisie who spoke this time.

"Beth, honey, I've almost got lunch ready. Do you want me to bring it to you on a tray?"

"You'll do no such thing!" Pete roared. "She'll eat it at the table like the rest of us."

All four outside her door engaged in an argument about the etiquette of dining at the noon hour until Liz wanted to scream. Who cared about lunch? After the morning she'd had, food was the last thing on her mind.

Finally she couldn't bear their squabbling any longer. "Stop!" She shouted with all the imperiousness a princess should have and was shocked at the immediate silence.

"I will, of course, come down for lunch, Maisie. But I need a few minutes to freshen up. If you could convince the…the gentlemen to go away, I would be grateful."

"Well, 'course they'll give you time to freshen up, honey. You come down in fifteen minutes."

"Yes, thank you, Maisie."

She didn't move until, after Maisie's stern lecture, she heard everyone walk away from her door.

With a sigh of relief she sank down on the big bed.

She had a problem and she needed to come up with a solution now, before she had to face Lord Peter Morris again.

The princess's future husband was a virile, sexy man. It was easy to see why the princess had agreed to this marriage, even though she didn't think the two affianced people had much in common.

If the princess had ever kissed Pete, Liz was surprised she'd been willing to let another woman within a hundred yards of the man. She knew she wouldn't want another woman kissing him if he were hers.

But he wasn't.

And that was what she had to remember.

She had to ignore the desire, the need, that filled her every time he touched her. Dansky and Petrocelli would want her promise she wouldn't indulge in such...such paradise again.

For her own sanity she had to promise.

And Princess Elsbeth was an idiot!

She stood and went into the bathroom to wash up, leaving her hat lying on the bed. She wasn't sure she'd even get to wear the cream-colored Stetson, because she thought it might be best to hide in her room for the rest of her visit. It would be the easiest way to resist Pete's charms.

And he had a lot of them, in spite of his gruffness.

That thought brought a question. If he was so attracted to her he couldn't keep his hands off her— and that would seem to be true based on his behavior—why did he act as if he wished she was anywhere but here?

After all, he'd agreed to marry her.

Concentrating on the puzzle of Pete's behavior eased Liz's concern about her own.

Until her bedroom door opened and Pete stepped in, a glare on his face, his hands on his hips.

Chapter Five

Pete's gaze covered every inch of her. Which was almost as good as holding her. Almost.

His frown deepened as she gasped and backed away. Had he frightened her?

"I came to apologize," he said abruptly, without any softness.

She didn't say anything.

"I shouldn't have kissed you like that in front of everyone." He searched her face for some response, but other than staring at him with big green eyes, she didn't move. Suddenly he frowned and asked, "Why didn't you buy a green shirt?"

His switch of subjects got more reaction. She stared down at the blue plaid shirt and then back at him. "I like blue."

Those husky tones shivered down his spine and he stepped closer. She backed into the bathroom.

"I'm not going to hurt you," he said. He didn't enjoy feeling like a monster.

She licked her lips, and his gaze followed the small pink tip of her tongue with outrageous hunger.

"I...I think we should keep our distance from each other."

He stepped closer, reaching the end of the bed. "Why? Aren't engaged couples supposed to use the engagement to find out if they're compatible?"

"No! I mean, I think we know we're compatible."

"Come on, Princess. Don't expect me to believe you're inexperienced. I may not live in Europe, but your reputation has even made it here to America."

She blinked several times as if his words had shocked her. "The printed word is not always the truth."

With his gaze focused on her lips, he moved closer, muttering, "You sure as hell don't kiss like a virgin."

"Please!" she cried, extending her hand palm up to prevent him from coming any closer.

As if that would stop him.

"My lord!" Dansky protested from the doorway.

Pete closed his eyes, letting his head roll back. Then he turned to look over his shoulder. "Dansky, this is a private conversation. Go away."

"No, my lord! Her Highness—"

"Maisie is waiting to serve luncheon," Petrocelli said, entering the room behind Dansky. "Are you ready to dine, Your Highness?" he asked, extending a hand toward Beth. She didn't hesitate to rush to his side. He swept her in front of him and the two of them exited the room, leaving Pete and Dansky staring at each other.

Frustrated, Pete glared at his adversary. "You two aren't planning on living with Beth after the marriage, are you?"

"We will do as the king orders, my lord."

The man's stiffness told Pete his question had been inhospitable, but he didn't care. "Then I'll have a word with my future father-in-law," he snapped, and stormed out of the room.

Only as he was descending the stairs did he realize, for the first time, he'd admitted the possibility of the marriage taking place.

SEPARATED BY A TABLE and surrounded by Dansky, Petrocelli and Maisie, Liz felt more comfortable being with Pete. "Are we going to ride this afternoon?"

He looked up from his plate, eyes narrowing. "Sure, I'll take you for a ride. There are some special places I'd like to show you."

"We will enjoy seeing more of your ranch," Petrocelli agreed with a smile.

Pete stiffened. "I believe the princess and I can manage a ride without your company. Harvey can show you around if you want to see the ranch."

Three no's rang out.

Dansky was the first to elaborate. "His Highness warned us to keep Her Highness safe, my lord. We cannot allow her to ride without our protection."

"She is a neophyte with horses, sir," Petrocelli added.

Liz decided she didn't need to fight this particular battle. Her two protectors would handle it. She took another bite of mashed potato.

Pete gave each of them, including Liz, a hard stare before returning to his meal. He said nothing else, but Liz didn't think he'd accepted the circumstances.

"My, Beth, you look just like a regular cowgirl in your new duds," Maisie said, probably hoping to distract Pete.

"Thank you, Maisie. I find the blue jeans amazingly comfortable. Before I leave I may have to buy several more pairs."

"A princess in blue jeans?" Pete scoffed. "I'm sure your father will have something to say about that."

How could she respond? She didn't know her supposed father. And if the king was willing to force his daughter into a marriage she didn't want, could Liz assure Pete he would allow her to wear what she wanted? She doubted it.

She was beginning to think being a princess was no picnic.

"His Highness does not object to casual dress on appropriate occasions," Dansky said.

"Does the king realize that once Beth marries me, she'll be under my rule, not his?" Pete asked, his jaw squaring.

Before Dansky could counterpunch, as everyone could see he intended to do, Liz rose from the table. "While you two gentlemen are determining my destiny, I shall return to my room to fetch my hat and gloves. Excuse me."

Behind her she heard Maisie's calm words. "I think you men have a lot to learn about women."

"HAVE YOU NO English saddles?" Dansky asked.

"Nope. This isn't a riding school. We only have Western saddles," Pete explained with singular disinterest in the man's wants. In fact, he hoped the two escorts would refuse to ride.

Petrocelli took the reins of the horse one of the cowboys led to his side. "We will manage," he assured Pete.

"Well, that's a big relief," Pete muttered under his breath. "Go ahead and mount."

"We must first assist Her Highness," Dansky returned.

"What do you think I'm going to be doing? That's my job."

"No, my lord, it is—"

"I told you to stop using my title!" Pete snapped.

"But—"

Beth's musical tones interrupted as she arrived at the barn. "Must you three always bicker?"

Pete and his adversaries turned to stare at her, but the cowboys in the area all rushed to Beth's side, each greeting her like a best friend. Pete shook his head in disgust. If last night hadn't convinced him, he recognized today that his cowboys weren't going to help drive Beth away.

His jaw tightened. The surge of protest that rose in him at the thought of her leaving was a surprise. What was wrong with him? He couldn't marry a princess, some prima donna determined to take him away from his beloved ranch.

The only problem was, princess or prima donna, neither title seemed to fit Beth.

While he'd stood and stared, Harvey brought forward the mare Pete had picked out for Beth.

"Here's your horse, Beth," he said, offering her the reins.

To Pete's amazement, she took the reins with a smile, then rubbed the mare's nose and forehead. "What a beauty. Is she well trained, Harvey?"

"Yes, ma'am. All our horses are. And she's got the sweetest gait you'll ever see. Her name's Beauty." He ducked his head and grinned. "We thought that was a good name for *your* horse."

Pete watched in amazement as Beth leaned forward and kissed the old cowboy's cheek. "Thank you, Harvey."

"I chose her for you," Pete said gruffly. It wasn't fair for Harvey to get all the credit. And the kiss.

"Shall I boost you up, Your Highness?" Petrocelli asked.

"That's not necessary with a Western saddle," Pete said. "She can pull herself up with the saddle horn."

"But the princess is used to mounting with assistance," the escort said.

"Then I'll do the assisting."

"No, Pete, it is my duty to—"

"I insist—"

"I must—"

"Gentlemen," Beth called, and Pete swung around to see that she'd been seated on the mare while they'd argued. "Harvey assisted me."

He glared at his old friend and then realized how unfair he was being when Harvey looked at him in confusion. "Thanks, Harvey."

"No problem, boss. Shall I ride with you?"

Pete rolled his eyes. "No, I think the princess already has enough escorts." More than enough. "Mount up, gentlemen."

Dansky managed to mount his horse fairly gracefully, but Petrocelli, shorter and rounder, had some difficulty. Pete glanced Beth's way and caught a glimmer of humor in her eyes, but she quickly hid it when Petrocelli looked up.

Maybe having escorts was a good idea. Pete needed to get to know Beth, and without the two men he might've abandoned that idea for more exciting things. Like kissing her.

LIZ LOVED being in the saddle again. But she couldn't relax. She had to maintain a rigid back like European riders, rather than loll in the saddle like Pete.

"Loosen up, Princess," the cowboy ordered, pulling in his horse to ride alongside her.

Oh, how she wanted to! "I beg your pardon?"

"We don't ride like we've got a poker stuck down our jeans."

She looked at Petrocelli and Dansky, both approximating her own posture. They urged their horses closer till the four of them were riding abreast.

"Is anything wrong?" Petrocelli asked.

"I was instructing the princess to relax."

Dansky frowned. "The princess is showing excellent posture."

"Yeah, but if she's going to stay in the saddle more than half an hour, she'll wear herself out."

"The princess has not ridden in some time. She should not overextend her energies the first day."

When Pete opened his mouth to counter, Liz interrupted. "Please. Do not argue again. I'm sure I shall adjust to your Western style of riding eventually, Pete, but it may take a little time."

He grunted, in agreement she thought, and maneuvered their horses toward a trail that led up into the foothills. Over his shoulder he said, "We'll need to ride only two abreast here because the trail narrows."

Clearly he intended her to ride beside him as he squeezed the two men out. She looked behind her at the others and smiled. As long as they were nearby, she'd be all right.

"What do you like to do for relaxation?" Pete asked.

"Um, I like the theater. And opera." She hoped. While her escorts had filled her in on protocol, she had no real sense of the private princess.

"You're not going to see much theater or opera here in Montana."

"Um, well, I like to read." Surely that was safe enough.

"What kind of books?"

Great. If she said mystery, the princess was sure to hate them. "A variety."

"Ever read any lowbrow stuff? Like Tony Hillerman?"

"I don't consider Hillerman to be lowbrow. Or Dick Francis, either."

"You like Francis?"

"Of course. I love his mysteries about racehorses." She suddenly realized she'd been answering his questions as Liz Caine, not Princess Elsbeth. "I've attended Ascot numerous times," she improvised.

"Do these two follow you everywhere?" He gestured to their companions.

"The king is concerned with my safety."

"He doesn't have to worry about your being safe here. I'll take care of you."

She looked at his broad-shouldered frame, his determined jaw, the strength in his gaze, and knew he was right. He would protect her from any danger. Except the danger that lurked in her. He couldn't protect her from losing control in his arms.

"What do you do for leisure?" she hurriedly asked.

"There isn't much leisure on a ranch. I occasionally watch football. Sometimes baseball, but I don't want to waste the long days in the summer."

"I like baseball," she agreed with a smile. It faded when he stared at her.

"You like baseball? When have you seen it? Baseball isn't popular in Europe."

Oops. "Well, I've seen several games since I arrived here."

"I thought you just got to L.A. Sunday and flew here yesterday."

She was getting in deeper all the time. With a nervous laugh she said, "I meant the first time I arrived in the United States."

Though he frowned, he nodded in agreement and she breathed a sigh of relief. Until he spoke again.

"You're beginning to relax in the saddle."

She immediately stiffened.

"Hey, that was a compliment, not a complaint."

"Um, thank you."

"At least you don't hold your reins halfway to your chin like some riders. They always remind me of Ichabod Crane." When she didn't say anything, he added, "You have heard of Ichabod Crane, haven't you?"

"Yes, of course. He was in that story by Nathaniel Hawthorne." Would the princess know of American literature? Of course she would. She was educated. Dansky had told her the princess had attended Oxford.

"Right. Do you ever play chess?"

"Yes." Liz and her father had battled over the chessboard frequently. She only hoped the princess had a similar experience.

"Good. Tonight after dinner we'll play a game."

"All right, though you don't have to entertain me, you know. I realize you are not on vacation."

"I haven't been the most hospitable of hosts. It won't hurt me to entertain you a little." He smiled at her and Liz took a deep breath.

If he was going to be charming rather than a grouch, she was in real trouble. "It seemed to me you were not pleased with my arrival."

A roguish gleam appeared in his brown eyes. "You think I kiss all my guests when they arrive?"

She knew he was teasing her, but she wasn't going to give up the opportunity to get to the bottom of his behavior. "It seemed you were more intent on teasing me than welcoming me."

Though his cheeks turned a little red, he continued

to smile. "It was an enjoyable experience, whatever the reason."

"But I'm right, aren't I? You didn't want me to come?"

"Look, Beth—"

"Is everything all right?" Petrocelli interrupted, urging his mount closer.

Liz could've screamed. Just when she was about to get some answers from the cowboy, her escort had to intervene.

"Yes," she replied sharply. "We are fine."

"How much farther will we ride, Pete?" Petrocelli asked.

"Tired already?" he asked, easing his mount to a halt. "If you want to turn back, you can see the ranch house from here. You can't get lost."

"Petrocelli is concerned for the princess, Pete," Dansky said as if correcting Pete's impression. "She is not conditioned to long rides."

Pete turned to look at Liz, and she avoided his gaze, as well as those of the other two men. She desperately wanted to continue the ride, to enjoy the outdoors, to spend more time with Pete. But the message from her escorts was unmistakable.

"Probably it would be best if we curtailed our ride today, Pete," she said, still staring at her horse's ears. When she finally dared look at him, he was scowling in her direction.

"Do you always do what they want?"

She wasn't happy about what she was doing, but she didn't like his criticism, either. Her back stiffened even more. Staring down her nose at him, she assumed her most princesslike tone. "I wish to return."

"Fine!" he snapped, and swung his horse around without waiting to see if she followed.

The ride back was as cold as winter in Montana. Pete didn't speak and rode alongside Dansky, his arch enemy, rather than Liz.

Since Pete was in front of her, Liz could relax and enjoy the ride, abandoning her princess imitation.

"Be careful. He might turn around," Petrocelli said softly.

"I doubt it. I think he's angry with me."

"Definitely. Which is a good thing. He was becoming much too interested."

"Isn't he supposed to? They're going to marry." She was surprised at how much it bothered her to think about Pete in a loveless marriage.

Petrocelli, on the other hand, seemed unconcerned. "This is a marriage of convenience, Your Highness."

"Whose convenience?" she muttered.

Fortunately she was staring at Pete's back when he turned around, and she stiffened in the saddle at once.

"Looks like we've got company. You expecting anyone?" he asked, his gaze hard.

She looked at the house half a mile away and saw a couple of vehicles parked beside it. Shaking her head, she said, "I don't know anyone here. Surely they must've come to see you."

"I don't recognize the cars."

"You know everyone's car in Montana?"

His lips tightened. "Just about."

Before she could say anything else, he prodded his

horse into a gallop. Dansky's horse immediately joined the faster pace.

"Must we keep up with them?" Petrocelli asked.

Liz looked at the man beside her. He didn't maintain as good a form as Dansky, but he'd ridden credibly well. "Why not?"

"I fear I may not be able to walk tomorrow as it is. I'm not used to riding."

"Maybe you should leave the baby-sitting to Dansky in the future if horses are involved. We won't go as fast, but aren't you concerned about who's waiting for us?" Her gaze returned to the scene ahead of them.

"Dansky will handle whatever arises."

Liz nodded and held her mount to a canter, a comfortable gait that wasn't an all-out run. She enjoyed the ride, knowing Pete wasn't watching her.

When they drew near the house, she stiffened her back again, preparing for an audience. She and Petrocelli pulled their mounts to a walk just as Pete swiveled around to glare at her.

"Friends of yours?" he asked, gesturing to two men in front of him.

Liz was at a loss for words. Did Princess Elsbeth know these men? Were they personal friends?

Dansky spoke up. "I can assure you, Pete, these men are not friends of the princess. I have already told you—"

Suddenly there was a flash of light, and Liz realized that one of the men had pulled a camera from behind his back and was snapping pictures.

Before she could protest, however, Beauty reared,

startled by the flash. While she might've been able to control the animal given a little time, Pete grabbed the reins and pulled the horse down. Then he hauled her out of the saddle.

"Harvey!" he shouted. Shielding Liz from the camera, he moved toward the barn with both her and her horse. When Harvey emerged from the barn, Pete shoved Liz toward him and turned back to the strangers.

"What's up, boss?"

"Take Beth to the barn while I escort our visitors off my land."

The steel in his voice would have frightened tougher men than the two before him. Liz moved behind Harvey but urged him to wait. She wanted to see what happened.

"You have thirty seconds to get off my land...or I'll throw you off," Pete warned.

For once Dansky and Petrocelli were in agreement with their host and they didn't hesitate to range themselves alongside him.

"Hey, man, I'm just trying to make a living."

"How did you know the princess was here?" Petrocelli asked. His voice was so soft Liz wasn't sure she'd heard him accurately.

"There was a lady at a dance club in L.A. I thought she was the princess, but she told me the lady was here, visiting her fiancé. Are you going to marry Princess Elsbeth?"

The question was addressed to Pete, but he didn't bother answering. "Your thirty seconds are up!"

Chapter Six

One of the men put up his hand as if hoping to hold Pete off. "You touch me and I'll sue. Your house-keeper invited us in."

"I'd guess you didn't tell her who you really were," Pete returned, and was satisfied by the flush that crept up the man's pasty skin.

As Pete moved closer to the reporter, the photographer darted around him in Beth's direction, snapping another picture as she stood by Harvey. Rage boiled in Pete. How dare these men intrude on his ranch! He'd promised Beth she'd be safe here.

Pete lunged after the man and grabbed him, knocking his camera to the ground. Beth's mount retreated, shoving Beth against Harvey.

As Pete dragged the photographer back toward his car, he noted that Dansky and Petrocelli were offering a similar escort to the reporter. It was the first time the three of them had been in agreement since their arrival.

"Wait! My camera!" the photographer protested.

Pete ignored him, but apparently Harvey didn't, because he caught up with Pete and thrust the camera into the man's hand.

"Hold it, Harvey. Take the film out first," Pete instructed the cowboy. Under a howl of protest from the photographer, Harvey retrieved the camera and figured out how to open it. He pulled out a spool of film and spilled it into the sunshine.

"Good job." Pete smiled not only at Harvey but also Dansky and Petrocelli. Those two returned his smile before quickly retreating to Beth's side.

While the two unwanted visitors ranted and raved about their treatment, they also got into their cars and drove away. Pete didn't care what they threatened. He was on his own property, and they had no business being there.

He turned back to Beth, anxious to see if she was safe. Her two aides were huddled around her with an air of consternation, and Pete rushed over. "Is everything all right? You're not hurt, are you, Beth?"

All three turned horrified gazes to Pete, but Beth had a hand clapped over one eye.

"Did you hurt your eye? We've got a good eye doctor in town. I can take you in—"

"No!" she gasped, sounding as if she'd run a hundred miles. "No, but I lost my contact."

Pete frowned. "I didn't know you wore contacts. Did you hurt your eye at all?"

"No, but...I need to go to the house and find my spare set."

"You have a spare set?" Dansky asked, relief in his voice.

Something seemed strange about this entire scene,

Pete decided, studying first Dansky and then Beth. "You didn't know that?" he asked the aide.

"Dansky was on an errand for the king when Her Highness had her last eye examination," Petrocelli said as he took Liz's arm and began leading her to the house.

"Why are you covering up your eye?" Pete asked, his gaze never leaving Beth.

"Uh, it affects my balance when I only have good vision in one eye," she said, but Pete noticed she didn't look at him as she answered.

"Maybe I'd better check your eye just to be sure you didn't hurt it."

"No!" Beth, Dansky and Petrocelli all shouted at once.

"The light bothers my eye without the contact, so I'd better keep it covered," Beth added.

"We could look for your missing contact," Pete suggested, still studying the others. "If it's one of those tinted ones, it might be possible to find it."

Again, all three rejected his suggestion.

Yep. Something was definitely strange.

"I have to go inside right away," Beth said, clutching Petrocelli's arm. "Do you think those reporters have gone? Or will they return?"

"If they've got any smarts, they'll leave and never come back," Pete said, his voice hard. "I'll call the sheriff and warn him about them."

"Come along, Your Highness," Petrocelli urged. Dansky, too, seemed intent on getting the princess inside.

Pete gave instructions to Harvey about their horses and then hurried after the trio.

He'd been angry that Beth wanted to end the ride, but that didn't mean he should ignore her needs. She would have trouble walking if losing her contact affected her balance. The least he could do was help her.

Ignoring the anticipation that rose in him at the thought of holding her again, he caught up with them and scooped Beth into his arms.

It thrilled him when, with a shriek, her arms circled his neck, her hands touching his skin, sparking memories of their earlier embraces. He grinned down at her, ignoring the aides' protests—and came to an abrupt halt.

She'd forgotten to keep her eye covered during his surprise move. Now he understood why shielding that eye had been so important. It wasn't the same color as the other one.

Staring down at her, he demanded, "Maybe you'd like to explain why one eye is green and the other blue?"

LIZ HEARD the gasps from her escorts, knowing they feared the deception had been discovered. But she was determined to carry on.

"I'll be glad to explain if you'll put me down." It was too distracting to be held against his strong body.

"My lord—" Dansky began, but Liz cut him off.

"No, Dansky, I think Pete should be told the truth."

Since the man had no idea what Liz was going to say, he quieted at once, but his eyes spoke volumes.

Pete set her on her feet and stood before her, his hands on his hips, his jaw squared in determination.

"Well? I'm waiting."

She drew a deep breath and began the story she'd just made up. "The rulers of Cargenia have always had green eyes. My mother, however, has blue eyes. When I was born, my father thought nothing of my blue eyes because he expected to have more children, a son, to carry on as King of Cargenia. But my mother could not bear any more children. And my father loved her too much to divorce her."

She paused to draw a deep breath—and steal a look at her aides—before she continued. "When I was old enough, my father explained the problem and suggested I wear colored contacts to hide my deficiency."

Pete stared at her, a ferocious frown on his face, and she waited for his reaction.

Finally he said, "That's it? You wear contacts to satisfy some silly tradition?"

In true royal attitude, she stomped her foot. "It is not silly! Cargenia has never been ruled by a queen. I must meet the strictest requirements to be considered acceptable."

"I don't want you to rule your country, anyway. You'll be here!" Pete's jaw squared even more, if that were possible.

"Don't be ridiculous. I must rule Cargenia. There is no one else." She hoped she was right. She knew the princess was an only child.

"Please, my lord—" Dansky began, a soothing note in his voice that was rare for the man.

"Pete! You're supposed to call me Pete."

Liz hid a smile at Pete's reaction. But it also gave her pause. He was determined to be an American cowboy, albeit a rich one, and nothing else. And yet he'd agreed to marry a royal princess, even one from a small country like Cargenia? It didn't make sense.

"What Dansky meant to say, Pete," Petrocelli said with an ingratiating smile, "is that Her Highness has no control over certain things. You must discuss these issues with the king."

"Fine! Let's go call him right now, because I want it understood from the start that *if* this marriage comes off, I'm going to expect Beth to be my wife, not some ridiculous holder of the throne." Without waiting for anyone's agreement, he struck out for the house.

Liz stared at her accomplices, unsure what her next move should be. Suddenly she made up her mind and hurried after Pete. "No, Pete!"

"What?" he barked.

"Let's wait until I return home. It is important that I talk to my father in person. He…he does not like to discuss serious issues over the phone."

"But you might not explain things the way I want you to," he growled.

"You can trust Dansky and Petrocelli to explain exactly how you feel. After all, it is important that everyone is satisfied with our arrangement."

He stared at her for several minutes, his gaze trying to penetrate her head, to discover her secrets. Liz hoped he couldn't, or there'd be disaster all around. Finally he nodded.

"Okay. But no more contacts while you're here. I don't like dishonesty, so here you'll be blue-eyed." When she said nothing, he added, "You got that?"

Liz looked at Petrocelli and Dansky for agreement. She would prefer to forget the contacts, but she wasn't sure how her protectors would feel about such behavior.

They both nodded slightly.

"All right. And you'll wait and let me talk to my father first?" She wanted to emphasize that point. After all, she couldn't agree to anything that would commit the princess.

Pete suddenly grinned at her, taking her by surprise. Wrapping an arm around her shoulders, he moved her in the direction of the house as he said, "I'm thinking it might be best if I go back to Cargenia with you when you leave. Then we can talk to the king together."

Liz's knees crumpled beneath her.

As soon as Pete had carried Beth to her room, ignoring her protest that such action was unnecessary, he retreated to the kitchen and called the local doctor.

There had to be a reason for her fainting, and he wasn't about to be accused of negligence. Probably it was all the tension created by those reporters, plus the jolt she took from Beauty bumping into her, but he wanted to be sure.

"Is the princess all right?" Maisie asked, concern in her voice, as he hung up the phone.

"I think so, but I want Doc to check her out. She's going to rest for a while, and he'll be here in about an hour."

"Shall I take her something to drink? Maybe a cup of hot tea. Do they drink tea in Cargenia?"

"How the hell should I know, Maisie?" he grumbled. His mind was on the woman upstairs, not the eating habits of her countrymen.

Maisie's eyebrows shot up. "Someone is worried, I think. Good. That will please your mother. Oh, she's arriving at the airport in Helena at ten this evening. I told her you'd meet her."

Damn. That was the last thing he needed. He was confused as it was. He didn't need the added pressure of his mother's watchful eye.

His idea in the beginning had seemed so simple. He'd set out to chase the princess away, to weasel out of the agreement. After all, the ranch was his life and he'd do whatever it took to keep it.

Every year as a boy he'd merely existed at school, holding his breath for the three months of the year he really lived— here on the ranch. His grandfather had taken him with him everywhere, teaching him to ride, to handle cattle. He'd had Harvey, a formidable cowpoke in his day, teach him how to swing a rope.

Pete had always known this ranch was where he belonged. Now he was looking for ways to make the promise he'd made his mother work. Beth had wormed her way into his life, though he wasn't sure how. The kisses hadn't hurt. Her charm, too.

The memories he had of his earlier brief meetings with the princess had prepared him to dislike her. But though she was sometimes regal, she was never rude. Though she wasn't used to everyday ranch life, she never looked down on it. She brought a vibrancy to him he hadn't even realized he was missing.

And he wasn't as sure now that he wanted it, or her, to go away.

But he also had no intention of being involved in the ruling of Cargenia. Neither would his wife—whoever that turned out to be.

What was he going to do?

"I'll go tell Beth the doctor is coming." He hurried out of the kitchen, afraid Maisie might recognize his dilemma. And he knew she'd tell his mother.

That would *really* be the last thing he needed.

"A BRILLIANT RECOVERY, Your Highness," Petrocelli whispered once the door closed behind Pete.

Liz frowned as she rethought her story. "But will it harm the princess? He will expect her to have blue eyes when he sees her in the future. It'll be an instant giveaway."

"You had no choice, Your Highness," Dansky assured her. "You either had to confess our duplicity or do what you did. I admit I thought our deception was ended."

"Perhaps that would've been better. I'm coming to hate what we're doing. Pete shouldn't be…misled like this." It wasn't fair, what the three of them were doing. Pete was too good a man to be a pawn in some scheme to pump money into the princess's country. After her time in California, she'd begun to believe there were no men like Pete left in the world—strong, honest, dependable men.

Dansky stiffened. "I can assure you the engagement was arranged as a marriage of convenience, both the princess's and Lord Peter's. His family felt the match would enhance his standing."

Somehow those words didn't sound like Pete. Not a man who disdained his own rightful title in England to become a cowboy in America. Liz lay back against the pillows, frowning. She needed to get to the bottom of the puzzle of Pete's agreement to the marriage.

Not that it was her business of course, but—

A knock on the door interrupted her thoughts. She turned alarmed eyes toward her guards.

Petrocelli sent her a comforting smile and turned to the door, opening it only a little, so Liz couldn't see who had knocked.

But she knew. Somehow, whenever he was within shouting distance of her, she knew Pete was there.

Petrocelli was whispering, so Liz had to wait until the door closed and her visitor retreated before she could discover the reason for Pete's return.

"Well?" she asked when Petrocelli turned back toward the bed where she waited, a frown on her face.

"He has insisted on calling the doctor. He wants to be sure you are not injured."

"Really! I told him I was all right."

"Your fainting alarmed him," Dansky pointed out.

She rolled her eyes. "I know that! But what else was I to do? His suggestion that he accompany me to Cargenia would create all kinds of problems."

"You will submit to the examination," Petrocelli

decided, sounding as if he'd come to a decision. "That will prove to Pete you are all right. And Dansky must return to L.A. to find the princess."

"What?" Liz shrieked.

Dansky, too, was surprised. "Why?"

"Because it was clearly the princess who sent the reporters. And because the situation here is...not what we expected. You must tell the princess of Pete's reaction. He is not treating this marriage as one of convenience."

Liz agreed. In fact, Pete's behavior was making the entire venture *in*convenient. Especially his kisses.

While she told herself to keep her distance—and had every intention of doing so—Pete made that resolve difficult to keep. She closed her eyes, but she couldn't hide from herself the jealousy that filled her, either.

She didn't want the real princess to come. To be in Pete's arms. To receive his kisses. In spite of five years in Hollywood, city of sin, Liz had refused to adopt its ways. She'd never found a man worth giving herself to.

The scariest thing about Pete was that she was beginning to think he filled that role. He might be worth giving her all. But she couldn't. Because she wasn't the real princess.

OVER DINNER that evening, which didn't include the cowboys as it had the night before, Pete said to Liz, "I'm going into Helena to pick up my mother this evening. Would you like to ride with me?"

Liz nearly choked on her baked beans. "Oh..."

She looked at Petrocelli, wondering what he would want her to answer.

"The doctor advised the princess to relax until the morning, Pete. I do not believe it would be best for her to go with you." Petrocelli added, "However, if Dansky might beg a ride with you, it would be most helpful. He needs to return to Los Angeles for a short time."

Since Petrocelli had already explained his plan to her and Dansky, Liz was prepared. Pete, however, seemed quite surprised. "L.A.? May I ask why?"

"A commission for the king," Dansky said smoothly, keeping his gaze on his dinner plate.

"You've talked to him?" Pete demanded.

"No, my lord, but—"

"There was no time before we left L.A.," Petrocelli hurriedly put in. "But now that we are assured of the princess's comfort here, Dansky felt he could be spared to take care of the chore."

Petrocelli was rivaling her in storytelling, Liz thought. Pete seemed grumpy this evening, but he accepted the man's tale.

"It's a long way to go, but I'll be glad to give Dansky a ride to Helena. Shall we leave here about seven or seven-thirty? Will that put you at the airport in time for your flight?"

"I will call the airlines as soon as dinner is over. If not, I will stay in a hotel and leave the next morning," Dansky assured him.

Feeling everything was in hand, Liz relaxed and cut another piece of her baked chicken.

"Sorry about the chess game, Beth," Pete said, looking at her. "We'll have to play tomorrow night."

"Oh, that's—"

"The princess does not play chess," Dansky interrupted.

Both Liz and Pete stared at the man. Liz tried to make a recovery before Pete. She returned her gaze to her plate, remembering she'd forgotten to ask the men about the princess's ability to play chess.

Pete scowled. "But she said she did."

"What Dansky means is I don't play chess well. He…he doesn't like for me to do anything if I don't do it well. A princess must be above reproach." She shrugged and smiled at Pete.

"That's ridiculous. We'll play and maybe you'll get better."

His patronizing attitude didn't please Liz. She was a good chess player, and she'd love to beat the socks off him. But now she'd have to plod along, pretend to be lost. Darn!

"While I'm gone, there are a lot of movies you can watch," Pete said, drawing her attention again. "We have quite a video library since entertainment isn't close at hand."

"That will be lovely," she said graciously, smiling at Maisie rather than Pete. "Would you join us, Maisie?"

"Well, I do love a good film. What kind do you like?"

The answer to the housekeeper's question was more unknown territory. Desperate, Liz looked at Petrocelli.

"The princess enjoys a good mystery."

Ah. She hadn't been that far off when she'd said she read mystery novels. At least she'd gotten something right.

"And I have a few books she might enjoy," Pete added, smiling at her.

As she was reveling in the warmth of his response, Dansky said, "The princess seldom reads."

Pete's smile vanished at once.

Liz was beginning to feel she was dancing on top of a stove, leaping from one hot spot to another. She hurriedly said, "I seldom have time to read. Only once in a while do I find myself without a commitment. Perhaps while I am here I will be able to read."

Though his gaze remained narrowed, focused on her, Pete nodded. "Good. I hope you feel comfortable here. And as long as the reporters stay away and your father remains in Cargenia, you should have some extra time."

"Yes." She smiled, but while her mind frantically dealt with the possibility of the king coming to Montana. That was a horror she hadn't yet considered.

"Of course once Mother arrives she'll occupy a lot of your time. She wants to get to know you better." Pete grinned at her, a teasing look that made her toes tingle. "It will help me if you keep her so occupied she can't drive me crazy, too."

"I'll do my best."

The rest of the dinner passed without any more contradictions or disasters. Liz was prepared to retreat to her bedroom until after Pete left, thereby avoiding any more quicksand, but he rose from the table and held out his hand.

''I'm going to have to leave in a few minutes. Let's take a little walk before I do.''

Petrocelli immediately protested again. ''No, Pete. The doctor said the princess needs to rest.''

''I'm not taking her mountain climbing, Petrocelli. I'm talking about a stroll down to the corral. I'm also talking about a little privacy,'' he said in warning as Dansky opened his mouth. ''We'll be in full view the entire time, but if either of you steps off the porch, I swear I'll deck you.''

Liz stared at her escorts. When they shrugged and shot her warning looks, she knew she was on her own.

With Pete.

Uh-oh.

Chapter Seven

Pete held Beth's hand as he led her from the house into the warm Montana evening. He gave a satisfied sigh. His land, his cattle…his woman? That thought shook him. Even if he and Beth married, she would never belong to him. She would always belong to Cargenia, eventually returning to rule it.

And she would marry him for his money. He must never forget that. In an attempt to put aside such unsettling thoughts, he smiled at Beth and said, "It's a perfect evening, isn't it?"

"The weather is certainly pleasant. Does it get very cold here in the winter?"

"Frigid," he assured her cheerfully. "But we can keep each other warm." His remark was intended to gauge her intent, and it fascinated him that she blushed. He'd assumed she'd be too sophisticated to do so. "You're not afraid of intimacy, are you?"

"No! Of course not. You…your words surprised me."

He squeezed her hand. "Winter may be hard here, but there's less outdoor work to do. I even manage some skiing. I know you're quite an experienced skier.''

She gave him a quick look and then turned to look at the mountains. "Mmm-hmm."

"Of course, our slopes won't seem like anything after the Alps. Which resort is your favorite?"

Instead of answering his question, she asked one of her own. "Have you skied the Alps?"

"A few times...when I was younger."

"Ah. Well, I like many different resorts."

"Okay. Are there any in Cargenia?"

She'd turned her gaze away from him again. Now she looked at him blankly. "Any what?"

What was wrong with her?

"Any ski resorts."

"Oh, uh, yes, I think...yes, there are several."

"You seem nervous. Is it because we're alone?" He'd suddenly realized this was their first conversation without the two guards hovering over them. Even when they were on horseback and couldn't be overheard, the men were still close.

She nodded but kept her gaze averted.

He reached out to take her by the shoulders. "Beth, I promise I won't attack you. I'd like to kiss you, but I won't if it..." He started to say, "if it frightens you," but then he remembered who he was talking to. Princess Elsbeth, party girl of Europe. Why would he think she'd be frightened by a kiss?

Catching her chin with his thumb and forefinger, he forced her gaze to his. "You're not afraid of a kiss. Not from the pictures I've seen of you. What's going on?"

"What do you mean?"

"Why are you acting like a shy virgin? Your reputation is well-known."

"So you've said, but I warned you. You shouldn't believe everything you read."

He thought about her warning. He'd certainly envisioned her life differently when he'd thought about it. Even after the strictures of his own life, as the son of a duke, he'd assumed that she, as a princess, would be able to do what she pleased. That thought reminded him of his earlier desire to rescue her.

"Look, Beth, once we—*if* we marry, you'll have more freedom. I won't let your father dominate you or allow those two apes to tell you what to do. You'll be a free woman."

His woman. One he could kiss without asking permission. Her skin would warm to his touch, her breath would mingle with his. Whatever her political persuasion, he already knew they were physically compatible. As his body was reminding him now.

Instead of responding to his offer of rescue as he'd thought she would, Beth stiffened and her chin rose several notches. "I do not need any assistance. I am already free."

"Sure you are," he retaliated in disgust. "You look to those two—" he nodded his head in the direction of the house "—before you answer any question. Your father tells you who you'll marry and how you'll spend your days. You can't move without reporters chasing after you. Yeah, you have a great life!"

Okay, so he wasn't being kind. But he was tired of

the restrictions that came with Beth. He was tired of her cooperating with them. And he was even more tired of not being able to hold her.

"I was born to this life. I have no choice, unlike the second son of a duke. I cannot choose to abandon my responsibilities."

"Hey, lady, I meet all my responsibilities. I don't shirk hard work. My brother doesn't need me to hang on to his coattails."

"And I do not need some rustic cowboy to rescue me from my life as a princess."

"Okay, fine!"

"Okay, fine!"

They glared at each other as if each faced the enemy. Yet Pete still wanted to kiss her. What was wrong with him?

"Pete?" Maisie called from the back porch. "Isn't it time for you to leave?"

"Yeah, it sure as hell is," Pete muttered, more as a warning to himself than a response. After all, Maisie couldn't hear him. With one last look at the stubborn but beautiful face before him, he spun on his heel and strode toward the house, not waiting for Princess Elsbeth to accompany him.

And that might be the only decision she got to make for the next ten years!

LIZ WATCHED PETE stalk away from her, regret filling her heart. She hadn't intended to antagonize him, but his questions cut away any confidence she had in playing her role. She'd never skied a day in her life—

Kansas was flat—and she wasn't familiar with any of the ski resorts in the Alps.

And she couldn't let him knock the princess's lifestyle. After all, the princess seemed happy with it.

Except, of course, for coming here, to meet her fiancé. It seemed both participants in this engagement were reluctant. So how could she encourage Pete to make the engagement real when she was sure the princess didn't want it?

And she suspected the same for Pete.

She leaned against the corral fence until she heard Pete's truck come to life, and then she watched it race down the long drive.

He was taking his truck to pick up his mother. Liz laughed, enjoying the release of tension. Pete obviously didn't stand on ceremony with his mother, even if she was a dowager duchess.

His lack of pretentiousness was just one of many things about Pete that pleased Liz. He was hardworking, good-natured—well, most of the time—and handsome as sin. When he forgot to be mad at her, he extended his protection to her, as he did to everyone on the ranch. And he loved his land.

Liz admired that in Pete. After her five years in Hollywood, rootless and surrounded by other rootless people, drifting from one job to another, Pete's roots were very attractive. His work was his life. Not even a princess could lure him away.

Not that she was a real princess. But she wished she was. She wished she could be whatever she had to be to find her place in Pete's embrace. To embed her roots with him here in Montana. To build a future together.

She blinked furiously to stop the tears that suddenly filled her eyes and forced herself to face facts. She wasn't the princess, she wasn't going to marry Pete, and she wasn't going to be able to do her job effectively if she didn't shore up her defenses against the handsome cowboy.

It was time to face reality.

"IS THE KING a reasonable man?" Pete asked his companion as he drove toward Helena in the gathering dusk.

Dansky turned questioning eyes to him. "I do not take your meaning."

"Look, Dansky, I know I agreed to this engagement, and…and, surprisingly, I'm no longer…that is, I think Beth and I can manage if we don't have complications from her father."

"His Highness wants his daughter to be happy."

"I'm sure he does, but is he willing to compromise on some of the duties in Cargenia? I can see visiting in winter when there's not so much going on around here, but spring and summer are definitely out."

"The princess will not be willing to stay on the ranch the entire year except for one visit in winter." Dansky stared straight ahead.

"I think Beth has adjusted very well to ranch life. Much better than I expected. What I'm asking is, will the king cut her some slack as long as she's happy?"

When he got no response, Pete took his eyes from the highway and looked at his passenger. "Well?"

Dansky seemed to be working under some duress. His lips moved several times. Finally he said, "I do not believe the princess will remain content. She is making an extra effort because…because she wants to please her father, but in general, she…she is easily bored."

Pete's eyes narrowed as he thought about Dansky's warning. True, he'd believed the same thing about Beth until she'd arrived. And maybe he was an idiot to be so easily convinced he'd been wrong. But the Beth of the past two days was warm, outgoing, friendly, patient. She'd won the hearts of his cowboys in no time flat.

She'd seemed content to ride. The scenery pleased her. She'd even seemed interested in his touch. Interested, hell! She'd reached for him eagerly once he'd initiated contact. No doubt about that. Physically she was more in tune with him than any woman he'd ever touched.

"I think you're wrong. Beth likes it on the ranch. She'll learn to love it as much as I do."

"The ranch is a novelty at the moment," Dansky countered. "The princess will change her mind."

"You seem awfully sure of that."

"I am, my lord. Very sure."

LIZ, MAISIE and Petrocelli sat in front of the TV, but none of them watched the movie playing on the VCR.

Liz glanced at her escort as he snored lightly on the opposite couch. She feared he'd be stiff tomorrow after their ride. At least he was getting some extra rest now.

Maisie, on the other hand, was knitting. Her needles clicked with steady regularity, her gaze seldom rising to the television.

"What are you knitting?" Liz asked softly. Her own mother frequently knitted and the sound was comforting to her.

"Baby booties."

Liz gave her a polite smile. "How nice. Someone you know is having a baby?"

Maisie looked at her, surprised. "I'm knitting them for your babies."

Liz sputtered out the iced tea she'd just sipped. "*My* babies?"

"Aren't you planning on babies?" The alarm in Maisie's voice told Liz that only one answer was acceptable.

"Um, I'm sure…that is, of course. There's no hurry, is there? I mean, I'm still young, and Pete is—"

"Time's a wastin'. That boy is thirty-two. He needs to be a daddy."

"Well, of course, but—"

"I bet your daddy wants babies, too. He'd like a grandson to sit on the throne someday, wouldn't he?"

How could Liz deny that suggestion? She had no idea, but it sounded likely. "Yes. And I'm sure we will if we… Babies are a possibility."

"I can knit those little sweaters and caps for the winter, too," Maisie offered enthusiastically, leaning forward. "You just give me the word and I'll start at once."

"Th-thank you. But I don't think it's necessary to start just yet."

Maybe she could convince Maisie to knit her a lifeline, because she was getting in deeper and deeper every minute.

"I'M EXHAUSTED. These transatlantic flights are so tiring. And then, of course, I had to fly from New York to Helena."

"Relax, Mother. You can doze all the way to the ranch if you like." Pete held his breath, hoping she'd take his suggestion.

"No, of course not. Robert sends his best, as I'm sure you know. Now, tell me about Princess Elsbeth."

"Nothing from Celia?" Pete asked, stalling. His brother's wife made her dislike for him all too clear, so he knew she wouldn't have sent him warm regards.

The dowager duchess's lips tightened. "The young woman gets above herself. After all, she's only the daughter of an earl."

"Uh-oh. Trouble in paradise?"

"You may joke, Peter, but I only had Robert's best interests at heart. I do not want him to be unhappy."

He knew his mother had wanted Robert's happiness, along with prestige and power. After all, Celia's father was a member of the House. The only difficulty was Pete's mother had never considered Robert's feelings. Only his position.

"That's why you should be careful promoting another match," he said softly, hoping his mother would take the hint.

She whipped her gaze to him. "You don't like her?"

Damn. He didn't want to answer that question. Not because he didn't know the answer. He liked her. Maybe even more than liked her when he held her against him. But liking her didn't mean he should marry her. Even if they had no personal difficulties, there would be obvious conflicts in their duties.

"The princess is a charming young woman, Mother, but she is the future ruler of Cargenia. She and her escorts are talking about my returning with her at various times during the year. I can't do that and run the ranch."

"Oh, piddle! You can hire a good manager. My father traveled the world and took me with him, and the ranch never faltered."

True. But he didn't want to be an absentee owner. He loved life on the ranch. He wanted to raise his children there. Not that he'd never take them anywhere, but… Damn it, he was thinking of his children as if he knew that one day—

"Have you talked to the princess about her responsibilities?"

"Not much. Those two goons are her shadows. When we're away from them, she acts like I'm going to attack her."

"Why would she think that?" his mother asked in surprise.

Pete felt his cheeks burn. He'd slipped up. "Uh, I…I've kissed her a few times."

"And she resists?" Lady Hereford asked, her brows rising in surprise.

His ego bruised, he responded with more emotion than he intended. ''No! She damn well doesn't!''

''Ah.''

He didn't ask her to explain what she meant by that, but he hurriedly reinforced his position. ''A few kisses don't mean anything. I've kissed more than one woman in my time, Mother, but I haven't married any of them.''

''And that is precisely why I have come. I shall be able to settle your differences and arrange a wedding.'' With a satisfied sigh she settled against the seat cushion and closed her eyes.

Pete didn't contradict her confident statement. In spite of himself, he almost wished his mother was right. If Beth could reject her princess status, simply be his wife, then he would willingly enter the marriage.

It suddenly occurred to him that without her status Beth wouldn't be his mother's choice. And with her status she wouldn't be his choice.

Would she?

LIZ WAS AWAKENED by the sound of boots descending the stairs. She checked the clock beside the bed and realized Pete must be going to work.

She'd expected him to sleep late this morning, after his trip to Helena. It had been after midnight when she heard the truck return, and she'd lain awake wondering what was going to happen this morning.

Petrocelli had told her she'd met Pete's mother only briefly on two or three social occasions. Nothing intimate or personal. With a grin Petrocelli had added that if she could handle Pete, the dowager duchess would be no challenge at all.

But then, Petrocelli and Dansky were also the ones who'd told her this week would be a breeze. "Just remain in your room and pretend to be a princess," they'd said. They couldn't have been more wrong.

She stayed in bed until she heard the distant thud of the back door as Pete left the house. Feeling safer, she pushed back the lightweight covers and slid from the bed.

A few twinges reminded her that it had been several months since she'd been on horseback, but a hot shower should take care of that discomfort. Petrocelli, on the other hand, would probably have difficulty walking.

Poor Dansky. He'd surely also have sore muscles added to the discomfort of a long flight. What would happen when he talked to the princess?

Liz froze as she considered the possibility that the princess might return with Dansky. Surely the woman would realize the impossibility of switching places. It would be so much wiser to wait until the week was over.

And it would give Liz a few more days to spend with Pete.

You're losing control, she warned herself.

With a sigh of acknowledgment, she headed for the shower.

A few minutes later she went down the stairs, wondering if she'd have a reprieve from meeting Pete's mother. Surely after a long flight the woman would sleep in.

"Good morning, Your Highness," a strange voice greeted her as she entered the kitchen.

With a sinking feeling, Liz knew there was no reprieve. She smiled and turned to an older woman, about Maisie's age, who rose and curtsied. "Good morning, my lady. How nice to see you again."

"Ready for your cup of coffee?" Maisie chimed in from the stove.

"Yes, please." Liz took a seat.

"Coffee?" the dowager duchess asked. "I thought you always drank tea."

Drat! Another mistake. Princess Elsbeth was going to have to make a lot of changes if she wanted to keep the switch a secret. "Maisie's coffee tempted me. I've come to enjoy it very much."

"In two days?" Lady Hereford's eyebrows soared.

"Now, Mary Margaret, don't you go giving Beth here a hard time. Why, she's been the best guest, as sweet as pie."

"I'm delighted of course, since it signals her willingness to continue with our agreement. But I will admit to surprise. I feared you wouldn't be able to adjust to life in Montana. It is quite different from the European lifestyle," she added with a shudder.

Liz was tempted to tell the woman what she could do with the European lifestyle *and* her fake English accent, but she restrained herself. After all, the dowager duchess was going to be Princess Elsbeth's mother-in-law. Wasn't she?

"I find life here quite charming," she said simply.

"Wait until winter. I agree, it's charming in good weather, but after you've stared at the walls for two weeks and it keeps on snowing, you'll go crazy." She pushed her cup toward Maisie as the housekeeper brought Liz her coffee. "I'll take another cup, too, Maisie."

Much to Liz's relief, the sound of someone else coming down the stairs caught the woman's interest. "Is this one of your escorts? Pete told me about them."

It didn't sound as if Pete had been too complimentary, Liz decided. Oh, well, Petrocelli could handle the dowager duchess, she was sure.

He entered the kitchen and gave a half bow. Liz knew at once that she'd been right about his stiffness. Trying to hide his grimace, he greeted Pete's mother with great formality, which she returned, obviously reveling in it.

Why the woman preferred the cold formality of blue bloods to the casual warmth of Montana natives Liz couldn't fathom. If the princess was the same, then Liz had done her a great disservice.

"Sit down, Mr. Petrocelli, and I'll pour you a cup of coffee," Maisie offered with a grin. "Looks like you could use a pillow or two on your chair. Want me to find you one?"

"Not at all, Miss Maisie. I'll be perfectly comfortable." His face belied his words, but Petrocelli bravely settled in his chair and reached for the cup she offered.

As Maisie straightened, the phone on the wall by the swinging door rang. "That's probably Pete wantin' to know how everyone is this morning."

Liz tensed. She was eager to see him, but she knew

it would be best to avoid him. When she noticed the dowager duchess's eyes on her, Liz took another sip of coffee and tried to look nonchalant.

Maisie's voice changed as she received a response to her greeting over the phone. Liz saw the housekeeper's gaze travel around the table to Petrocelli.

"I was wrong," Maisie said, holding out the receiver to the man. "It's Mr. Dansky."

Chapter Eight

Pete quietly stepped into the kitchen as Petrocelli took the phone from Maisie. As he removed his cowboy hat, Pete watched Beth. She seemed alarmed, or at the very least, concerned about something.

Had his mother upset her?

But she was watching Petrocelli as if he was the center of her difficulties. Was the king on the phone?

"Morning," he said softly, and watched Beth's gaze rivet on him with no hesitation. A smile slipped across his lips without conscious volition. She looked good enough to eat.

"Aren't you going to greet your mother?" the dowager duchess interrupted.

With a chuckle Pete bent and kissed his mother's cheek. "Oh, yeah. Morning, Mother."

Then he circled the table and greeted Beth the same way, though his lips lingered against her warm skin just a little longer. "How are my sleeping beauties?"

Maisie offered a mug of coffee and he took it before sitting down beside Beth. "Who's calling so early in the morning?"

Only Maisie spoke up. "Mr. Dansky is calling from Los Angeles."

Pete's eyebrows soared. "Then he really got up with the chickens. It must be six in the morning in L.A. Something wrong?" He looked at Beth for an answer.

"I...I don't know. We'll have to wait until Petrocelli finishes his conversation."

He noticed her fingers clenched around the coffee mug. If it had been a person, it'd be dead from strangulation by now. "Expecting bad news?"

"No! Of course not. I mean, I'm sure everything... Probably Dansky had a question about my...my father's request."

"Is anything the matter?" Lady Hereford asked. "I spoke with your father just before I left England. He seemed pleased with your willingness, Your Highness."

"Don't call her that," Pete rapped out without thinking. But he didn't like being reminded of the princess's responsibilities in Cargenia.

His mother's gaze widened. "Why ever not? That's the proper way to address her."

"I know, but here she's called Beth. If we're going to be family, it seems stupid to do otherwise."

Before anyone could argue with his logic, Petrocelli hung up the phone and turned around to find all eyes trained on him. "Uh, Dansky has completed his mission and will be returning this afternoon."

"I'll send someone to meet his flight," Pete offered.

"No, no, that is not necessary. He will hire a car."

Petrocelli hesitated and then turned to Beth. "May I have a word with you in private, Your Highness?"

Pete reached out and captured Beth's hand as it lay on the table. "We're all friends here, Petrocelli. Beth probably wouldn't mind if you spoke in front of us."

Beth's chin rose, as it always did when she was her most regal, and Pete admired the stubborn tilt of her chin. It distracted him briefly.

"I cannot discuss the business of my country in front of everyone, Pete. I know you will understand."

With a rueful smile he stared into her green eyes and... Green eyes? "Wait a minute. You and I have something to discuss, too. About your eyes!"

Alarm sprang into her gaze and she tried to tug her hand free. "Please, Pete, I will explain. Do not—"

"Why not?"

"Wait for my explanation, please?" Her pleading was more a question than an order, and he couldn't help but give in. After all, it was no big deal if he waited a few minutes without mentioning her eye color to his mother.

"All right. I'll expect an explanation. In private," he added with emphasis. He hoped she understood he'd want more than words when he got her alone.

But she gave no indication of his meaning. With another tug she freed her hand, rose from the table and led Petrocelli out of the room.

"How peculiar," his mother murmured.

"What?" he asked, his brow furrowed, his gaze still on the door through which Beth had disappeared.

But his mother didn't respond. She merely shared a secretive smile with Maisie.

"WHAT IS IT?" Liz asked as soon as the door to her bedroom had closed behind them.

"Dansky has talked with the princess, but she refuses to end our charade."

Air whooshed out of Liz and she slumped limply against the wall. "You mean we are to continue?"

"We must or be revealed as charlatans."

"Did Dansky explain that Pete...Lord Peter is taking the marriage seriously?" Liz thought that was a tactful way to detail Pete's behavior.

"Dansky tried, but the princess failed to grasp the gravity of the situation." Petrocelli frowned, worrying his bottom lip with his teeth. "Dansky is quite beside himself. He even went so far as to condemn the princess's behavior. I was correct that she gave the reporters our location because she did not want to cut short her week of freedom."

Anger rose in Liz. "That was charming of her."

Petrocelli stiffened. "I agree that the princess should not have done so. However, you were hired to work for a week and have been paid for that much time. It cannot matter to you."

"I was to stand in for the princess in a formal situation, to avoid the press. I didn't know anything about an engagement and you know it!" But Liz felt guilt building in her. How long could she continue to pretend to Pete, to mislead him so greatly?

"We must not argue. We must stand united."

Liz turned her back. She was even becoming fond of Dansky and Petrocelli, which was ridiculous since they'd gotten her into this mess. She couldn't say anything.

"Please, Miss Caine, you cannot abandon us now."

He reached out and touched her shoulder, and Liz turned back to face him. It was a measure of his desperation that he used her real name.

"I know, Petrocelli, I know. I made my bed and now I must lie in it."

"But not with Pete!" Petrocelli interjected, alarm in his words.

Her cheeks flamed. "That was a figure of speech. I didn't mean I intended to— Of course not!" The images that rose in her mind were wanton—and tempting. She shook her head.

"Very well. We will continue as we have. You must avoid being alone with Pete."

"I have to meet with him about my eyes. He noticed I was wearing the contacts again."

"Yes, why did you? I thought we agreed—"

"His mother. She met the princess and believes her eyes are green. I thought the fewer people who know of our difficulty the better. If Pete refuses to accept the princess, then he will explain to his mother. If he goes ahead with the marriage, the princess will be saved useless explanations."

"Yes, you are right. Elizabeth Caine, you have been an excellent conspirator. Dansky and I will tell the princess of your service. I'm sure she will want to reward you."

Liz shook her head. "I've been paid. If we get through this charade, I think maybe we'd best forget everything that has happened."

She particularly wanted the princess to forget that

she, Liz, had kissed the princess's future husband and lusted after him in her dreams. Yes, that had best be forgotten by the princess.

And by Liz. If only she could.

PETE PACED the floor of the narrow hall at the foot of the stairs, his gaze swerving back and forth as he kept watch on the landing at the top of the stairs.

Another minute. That's all he would give Beth and Petrocelli before he raced to her room and pounded on the door. He didn't like all the time she spent alone with those two men. After all, she was a beautiful woman—and he was jealous.

He hated admitting such a weakness. Never before had he concerned himself with a woman's companions. But then, he'd never considered marrying another woman.

Movement alerted him and he turned eagerly to the stairs as Petrocelli appeared.

"Where's Beth?" Pete asked.

"She will be down in a moment. But I will be glad to answer any questions you—"

"Nope. I want to speak to Beth. Alone."

"But, Pete—"

Beth's voice floated down the stairs. "It's all right, Petrocelli. I told you I would speak to Pete."

Pete tried to control the satisfied smirk he felt on his lips, but Petrocelli's glowering told him he hadn't done a very good job. "I won't keep her long."

Petrocelli continued into the kitchen and Pete stepped closer to the stairs, reaching out for Beth's hand as she approached. "Come on. In here."

He led her into the front parlor where they'd first met. And his behavior was remarkably the same. No words. Just an embrace that said everything for him.

His arms wrapped around her, pressing her lithe form against him, and his lips descended to hers. Her reaction, however, was different. She didn't show any hesitation in returning his embrace. Her arms went around his neck and she opened her lips to him, meeting him more than halfway.

The sweetness of her kiss was what he'd hungered for, dreamed of. It was purer than fresh honey, more powerful than the strongest aphrodisiac.

And he never wanted it to end.

He broke away from her only to immediately seize her lips again from a different angle as he moved the two of them closer to the sofa. His hands memorized her every inch, caressing and stroking even as they shifted. When he finally reached his destination, he drew her down and stretched atop her, eager to leave no space between them.

She pulled back, gasping. "Pete, we can't..."

Rather than recapture her lips, his nibbled along her neck, reaching the V of her silk blouse. All the while his fingers were maneuvering buttons at great speed. It was his mouth reaching one breast that halted her protest.

But only for a minute. She gasped, "You wanted to talk—"

"No," he muttered, returning his lips to hers. Why would he ever want to talk when he could touch her, stroke her, kiss her? An incredible hunger that his body had only hinted at was erupting in him. He wanted to shuck his jeans, all his clothes, and feel her with every inch of skin he possessed.

A firestorm of desire made control impossible and he gave up any idea of talking.

LIZ COULDN'T BELIEVE how quickly she'd lost control of their private conference. Or how little she cared. Once Pete started kissing her, she had difficulty remembering why she should protest.

Oh, she tried. But it was an unfair contest. After all, she had to fight both Pete and herself. This man touched her in a way no man ever had. Being one with him would feel so right, so perfect, that any rational argument against it was lost. She felt him tugging up the skirt she'd worn to breakfast and realized she couldn't complain because she was busily unbuttoning his shirt. The need to feel his warmth from her head to her toes made her action seem perfectly reasonable.

His mouth returned to her breasts and she couldn't remember anything except that she wanted him. He was her hero, her prince, her—

"No!" she protested, suddenly shoving against his shoulders. Now she remembered. Prince, princess. Those two fit together. But *she* wasn't the princess. *She* might love his touch, but he was going to marry the princess. Not her.

"What's wrong, sweetheart?" Pete murmured.

Liz felt sick to her stomach at how close she'd come to betraying herself, the princess and most of all Pete by making love to him under false pretenses.

"Pete, we must stop."

"Why? We're going to be married. Remember?"

"Are we? I'm not sure you're committed to our marriage."

He buried his face against her neck and Liz had to tighten her control.

"Why do you say that?"

"I have some questions. And I do not think we should indulge in such…such activities until they are answered."

"Could we, uh, answer them later?" He was resisting her ineffectual shoves and his lips took hers once again.

In spite of the temptation, she twisted her mouth from his, almost crying with the effort it took. "No. And…and I must explain about my eyes."

Pete seemed to have lost all interest in her eye color. He protested as she pulled her blouse together. "I want to see you, Beth. You're beautiful."

"You must get up, Pete. Someone will come…"

"They'd better not. But we'll go to my room. You'll be more comfortable on a big bed, and I'll guarantee no one will bother us there."

"No. I cannot. There are difficulties…"

"We'll work them out," he promised, lifting himself slightly to look down at her.

Liz's guilt rose and tears filled her eyes as she stared at his earnest face. He really believed they would be husband and wife.

But she knew differently.

"No, Pete, not now. We must wait."

"Until the wedding? Why? I wouldn't be your first

lover. Why should I have to wait because we're to be married? That makes no sense.''

His words were logical and she had no answer. But she knew it would be a betrayal to him more than anyone. Since she had no argument, she used her heart. ''Please?'' she whispered as tears filled her eyes.

He stared at her and she held her breath. Then he pulled himself up and stood, turning his back to her.

Liz lay on the sofa, unmoving, stunned by his compliance with her wishes, filled with despair at her loss.

''Cover yourself up!'' he snapped. ''My jeans are too tight for me to keep them fastened for long.''

His harsh words brought her to attention and she hastily sat up, arranging her clothing. How could she have so forgotten herself, wantonly tempting him after she'd said no? Her cheeks blazed with embarrassment. ''I'm sorry.''

''I guess I should apologize, too. I didn't mean to lose control so quickly. And I'll answer any questions you have, but I don't see the reason to wait. We both want each other.'' He stopped and turned to her. ''Don't bother arguing with me. Your body's already betrayed you.''

Liz kept her gaze on her hands, clenched tightly in her lap. ''I know. That is why I apologized. I encouraged you.''

She dared peep up at him and caught a rueful grin on his beautiful mouth.

''That's big of you, Beth, but we both know I started it.''

Liz decided any more discussion about their recent

activities would only lead to trouble. She changed the subject. "I wore the contacts today because of your mother. It embarrasses me that I have this deficiency. I would rather it be our secret."

To her surprise he knelt down beside her. "Sweetheart, those blue eyes of yours wouldn't be considered a deficiency by any other woman in the world."

His tender support was almost her undoing. And also strengthened her resolve. It was bad enough that she was lying to him. To allow any greater intimacies would be an unforgivable betrayal.

She sniffed. "Thank you, but...please keep my secret. It cannot matter to your mother."

He stroked her cheek, sending shafts of pleasure through her. "No. Your eyes don't matter to my mother. I won't say anything."

"Thank you."

He stood and pulled her up beside him.

"Now, what are these questions you have about our marriage?"

Frantically she sought reasonable questions. Other than those of her betrayal. "I...I do not think we should plan a wedding until we have discussed the problems of Cargenia with my father."

"I don't care about Cargenia."

Afraid to delve into the unspoken emotions that filled their relationship, especially on her part, she hurriedly said, "That is our difficulty. I must care...and you do not. I cannot abandon my country."

"But what will be required of you?"

She didn't know. "Uh, we must discuss it with my

father. After I return to Cargenia, I will talk to my father. Then we will call you.''

His hands were rubbing small circles on her shoulders and she ached to feel them against her skin. He was driving her crazy with his touch.

''I still think I should go with you.''

''No! No, I must have time alone with my father. He…he can be difficult.''

Pete stared down at her. Finally he muttered, ''Okay. Are there other questions?''

His lips drew closer and she frantically searched for more. ''I do not understand why you agreed to this marriage. It has been clear from the beginning that you do not wish it.''

She knew how right her words were when he stiffened and his cheeks reddened. Before, his resistance had been only a theory, a hint that had hovered in her mind.

''Look, sweetheart, I just wasn't sure that we would get along okay. I mean, I hardly knew you. Now we don't have any doubt about our being, uh, compatible, do we?'' He leaned down to touch his lips to hers as if to emphasize his point, bringing a surge of renewed hunger that almost made her mind go blank.

''Why did you agree to the marriage if you didn't feel you knew me well enough to marry me?''

He stepped away from her, then paced to the window. ''That's not important.''

''I think it is.'' She was about to discover his secret. If Petrocelli interrupted them now, she would fire him. Then she realized how silly her threat was.

Pete was about to speak again when he frowned and looked intently out the window.

"What is it?"

"I thought I heard something."

"It was probably the wind."

"Yeah, maybe."

"Are you going to answer my question?"

He turned back toward her, his hands again going to her shoulders. "I guess I will. But you're not going to like the answer."

"Why not?"

"Because it makes me sound pretty materialistic. You see, my grandfather left the ranch to my mother. And she threatened to sell it out from under me if I didn't marry you. She has delusions of grandeur because my father was a duke."

"Would she do that? Sell the ranch?"

"In a New York minute."

"And if you marry me?"

"I get the deed to the entire twenty-five thousand acres as a wedding present."

All Liz's dreams of convincing Pete he loved her, instead of the real princess, dreams she'd scarcely acknowledged but had grown inside her until they couldn't be ignored, withered and died in an instant.

She might be able to compete against a royal blue blood, but she had no chance at all against Pete's beloved Montana ranch. And she couldn't let him sacrifice it even if he would.

Pain filling her, she bowed her head and closed her eyes. Pete took her chin between his thumb and forefinger and lifted her face to his.

"Hey, neither of us agreed to the marriage because of love. It's a business proposition. You're just as guilty as I am. After all, we both know you had your eye on my fortune."

Liz wanted to hotly deny his words, to proclaim her suddenly realized love, her willingness to marry him even if his mother disowned him. But she couldn't.

"Right?" he prodded.

She nodded and let her gaze drop, unable to face him.

"So, now we start even again. We each have our reasons for this marriage to come about. And maybe we'll find a few more. Not the least of which is this."

Before she realized his intentions, he covered her lips with his and she was again sucked into the maelstrom of passion his touch engendered.

Until a bright light flashed in their eyes.

Chapter Nine

"Damn!" Pete roared, and almost threw Liz aside as he rushed from the room.

Liz wasn't quite as fast at comprehending what had happened, but two men rushing away from the window, one carrying a camera, brought her up to speed. Their car was hidden behind some trees nearby and they reached it before Pete could catch up to them.

Liz thought Pete would give up the chase once the men were driving away, but she underestimated him. He jumped into a nearby pickup and followed.

Finally realizing she should contribute to the action, Liz rushed into the kitchen. "Petrocelli, those two men came back and took a picture. Pete's chasing them."

Petrocelli leaped to his feet, but his painful muscles slowed him down. "Is there a vehicle I can use?" he asked Maisie.

"Sure," the housekeeper replied. "I'll call one of the boys at the barn and he'll drive you."

While Maisie called, Petrocelli hobbled out to the

porch, then headed for the barn. Liz stood beside the door, unsure what her next move should be.

"What did they take a picture of?" the dowager duchess asked. "Something valuable?"

Liz had forgotten all about Pete's mother, the one who had engineered the marriage.

"Uh, no," Liz replied, while inside her the word *yes* was screaming to emerge. "It was a picture of the two of us."

"Oh! You mean the press? That's good. We want the wedding to have as much publicity as possible."

"We do?" both Maisie and Liz asked together.

"Of course. Your father needs the influx of capital that a romantic fairy-tale wedding will bring. Surely he explained it to you?"

Liz gulped. "Yes, of course, but I thought he meant more-normal publicity. I think these two were from one of those tabloids. They were here before."

Lady Hereford shrugged. "Publicity is publicity." She picked up her cup and sipped coffee with total unconcern.

"Too bad Pete don't feel the same way," Maisie muttered. "He's liable to wreck his truck tryin' to catch those guys."

Liz's heart contracted with fear. "Oh, no, he...he'll be careful, I'm sure." But she remembered how he'd sped down the driveway, driving much too fast, and feared Maisie was right.

Without another word, she raced up the stairs to her room, her fears and dismay filling her. Not only could the photo put their charade at an end, it might

GET A FREE TEDDY BEAR...

You'll love this plush, cuddly Teddy Bear, an adorable accessory for your dressing table, bookcase or desk. Measuring 5 1/2" tall, he's soft and brown and has a bright red ribbon around his neck – he's completely captivating! And he's yours *absolutely free*, when you accept this no-risk offer!

AND TWO FREE BOOKS!

Here's a chance to get **two free Harlequin American Romance® novels** from the Harlequin Reader Service® absolutely free!

There's no catch. You're under no obligation to buy anything. We charge nothing – ZERO – for your first shipment. And you don't have to make any minimum number of purchases – not even one!

Find out for yourself why thousands of readers enjoy receiving books by mail from the Harlequin Reader Service. They like the **convenience of home delivery**…they like getting the best new novels months before they're available in bookstores…and they love our **discount prices!**

Try us and see! Return this card promptly. We'll send your free books and a free Teddy Bear, under the terms explained on the back. We hope you'll want to remain with the reader service – but the choice is always yours! (U-H-AR-05/98) **154 HDL CF5W**

NAME

ADDRESS   APT.

CITY   STATE   ZIP

Offer not valid to current Harlequin American Romance® subscribers. All orders subject to approval.

NO OBLIGATION TO BUY!

If offer card is missing write to: Harlequin Reader Service, 3010 Walden Ave., P.O. Box 1867, Buffalo, NY 14240-1867

BUSINESS REPLY MAIL
FIRST-CLASS MAIL   PERMIT NO. 717   BUFFALO, NY

POSTAGE WILL BE PAID BY ADDRESSEE

**HARLEQUIN READER SERVICE
3010 WALDEN AVE
PO BOX 1867
BUFFALO NY 14240-9952**

NO POSTAGE
NECESSARY
IF MAILED
IN THE
UNITED STATES

also put Pete at risk. Liz shook her head in disbelief. How had her life gotten so complicated?

Maybe Pete would catch the trespassers and expose their film. Or maybe her face had not been visible. While she resembled the princess very closely, anyone who knew her well—like the king—might easily realize the picture was not of the princess.

Then everything would be at risk.

PETE AND PETROCELLI entered the kitchen together more than two hours later.

"You okay?" Maisie asked.

"Yeah. The truck's a mess, though. I slid into a ditch. Where's Beth?"

Maisie fussed over him, as he'd known she would, but she also answered his question. "In her room. Pacing the floor worryin' about your sorry hide."

Pete left the kitchen without answering, eager to reassure Beth. He knocked on her door.

She swung it open and then threw herself into his arms. "You're okay!"

He hugged her close, enjoying the reward for his efforts. Unfortunately he had to tell her he'd been unsuccessful. "Yeah. Just a few bruises. But I didn't catch them."

"Bruises? Why? Did you get into a fight?"

"Yeah, with a ditch."

She reacted much the way Maisie had, searching him for injuries with her hands and her eyes. "Are you hurt? Shall we call a doctor?"

He wrapped his arms around her. "Nope. I'm okay. And the truck will be, too, in a couple of days. Since you sent Petrocelli after me, I wasn't left to wait long. Thanks.''

''What happens now?'' she asked, her face buried against his chest.

With his body reacting to her closeness in its usual way, the answer Pete would've preferred to give wasn't acceptable, he knew.

''Nothing much until that picture they took surfaces. Then we'll sue the pants off them for trespassing.'' He ducked his head and nibbled along her slender neck.

She abruptly pulled from his arms. ''We mustn't do this, Pete. Remember?''

''I remember your telling me we had to wait. But I don't remember understanding. You want to run those arguments by me again?''

''We both know there are problems with our...our marriage. I think we should wait until you have an opportunity to talk to my father before we do anything to...to commit ourselves.''

''And all those other men you've slept with were committed?'' He hated the sound of jealousy in his voice. He'd prefer to make Beth think he was sophisticated.

''There haven't been that many!'' she snapped, her cheeks flaming.

Pete narrowed his eyes as he studied her. ''How many?''

''None of your business! It's not like you're pure as the driven snow.''

''But I'm not the one refusing to share a bed.''

''So it all comes down to sex? Is that it? You want

sex, therefore I should provide it? Sorry, but I don't find that romantic! Please go away!''

She turned her back on him, leaving Pete to stare at her. Was she right? Was it simply a matter of sex? But he knew better even as he asked the question. There were women available. There always were for men with money, power or fame.

But he only wanted Beth.

Obviously she didn't feel the same. Pete wasn't going to wear his heart on his sleeve for anyone.

"So maybe I'll find someone more cooperative," he drawled, lying through his teeth. When she said nothing, he sauntered out of the room, waiting until he closed the door behind him to let his shoulders slump in dismay.

LIZ DIDN'T HAVE to face Pete again until dinner. She remained in her room until she was sure he'd left the house. Then she borrowed one of the books he'd offered the night before and returned to her bed.

In spite of a good story, she was anxious, even eager, to face him again, to see if he'd followed up on his last statement. Though she wasn't quite sure how she'd know. And if he had, she'd die a slow death.

It shouldn't matter to you, she reminded herself. *You're not going to marry him.* Which only depressed her more.

When Maisie called her to dinner, she'd showered and changed into one of her more casual dresses, as if the princess owned anything casual. It was a green silk shirtwaist that emphasized her faux-green eyes.

When she entered the kitchen, she discovered only Maisie and a table bare of dishes. "Didn't you call me for dinner?"

"Sure did. When Mary Margaret is here, dinner is always served in the dining room, with the good plates," Maisie explained, rolling her eyes.

A reluctant grin crept across Liz's lips. She didn't feel like smiling, but she couldn't hold back her appreciation of Maisie's words. "I see." She turned to go through the swinging door and then thought to offer her help. "Can I carry anything for you?"

"Lawsy mercy, child, Mary Margaret would have my head if I let you help. Go on ahead. I'll be there in a minute."

When she entered the dining room, she found her fiancé, Petrocelli and Lady Hereford standing by the cabinet where Pete had served drinks a few nights ago.

"Good evening," she said quietly, avoiding Pete's gaze after one quick glance. He was still angry with her.

"Evening," he drawled. The other two gave more effusive greetings.

Pete stepped forward and offered her a glass. "I found the white wine you wanted."

"Oh, I…" Petrocelli's warning look told her not to refuse. "Thanks."

"Shall we be seated? I believe Maisie is ready to serve dinner." Pete turned them all toward the table. Lady Hereford immediately assumed the foot of the table, where Liz had sat before, leaving side chairs for Petrocelli, Maisie and her.

Pete stared at Liz, as if he expected her to protest, but she moved around the table and took the chair next to Lady Hereford.

"Did you enjoy your rest?" the dowager duchess asked Liz, as if the princess's withdrawing from everyone's company for the afternoon was perfectly acceptable.

"Yes. I apologize for seeming unsociable, but the morning's events were...unnerving. Besides, I was reading a murder mystery and couldn't put it down."

Pete asked the name of the book, and a brief discussion of the plot ensued, making their relationship seem normal.

But Liz knew better. There was the same frostiness in his eyes that had been there that first day. Once she'd enjoyed the sparkling warmth of his gaze when he approved of her, Liz would never mistake this look for anything but censure.

After Maisie brought in the food and joined them, conversation was easier. Lady Hereford, of course, had not been there earlier to know her son and his fiancée had crossed over the lines of formality. Until she asked a question.

"What did those two get a picture of this morning? Beth seemed quite upset about it."

"I imagine she was," Pete drawled, sending one brief glance Liz's way.

"Surely you weren't doing something, er, unroyal?" his mother asked with a giggle.

With her gaze firmly fixed on her plate, Liz muttered, "We were embracing."

"Hugging?" Lady Hereford asked.

Liz couldn't believe the woman was asking for more detail.

"Nope," Pete replied, eliminating the necessity of a response. "I was kissing the stuffing out of her."

Lady Hereford beamed. "Wonderful! That will make wonderful press. But why did you follow them, darling?"

"Because I don't want my private life spread all over the world!" Pete snapped.

"But, darling, you know the king is hoping your marriage will stimulate their economy. It certainly can't be done in secret."

"I'm not sure it can be done at all."

Pete's growl was as painful as a knife, piercing Liz's heart. But she had a role to maintain. "We have come to the conclusion," she said, "that there are difficulties with such a marriage, my lady, and Pete must have the opportunity to speak face-to-face with my father before either of us can commit to it."

She looked up to see a grimness on Pete's face, surprise on Lady Hereford's and approval on Petrocelli's. At least everyone didn't hate her.

"But, my dears, the agreement has already been reached. Your Highness, you know your father has already begun laying the groundwork for the marriage. We have set the date for next March on your father's official birthday. I have already begun organizing the wedding, since you have no mother to assist you."

Liz stared at the woman, her mouth agape. The date already set? Somehow a definite date made her situation all the worse. After a quick glance at Petrocelli

Liz pursed her lips and said, "I will talk to my father."

Pete, after a hard look at Liz, drawled, "You have been busy, haven't you, Mother? Perhaps all to no purpose."

With unladylike frustration Lady Hereford pounded the table. "But you agreed!"

Pete drilled Liz with his glare again. "Complications have arisen."

"What complications?"

"I don't intend to participate in the ruling of her country. My job is here."

"You're being ridiculous!" his mother returned passionately.

"Am I? This is my life and I refuse to give it up. I would gain nothing by receiving the ranch if I can't live here."

"Well, of course you can live here. Several trips a year to Cargenia should satisfy them. Of course the princess will have to be there more often, but—"

"My wife will remain with me."

Liz kept her gaze fixed on her plate. She had no desire to enter this argument.

"You are being obstinate. Of course Princess Elsbeth must spend time in her country. She is to be its ruler one day."

A suddenly anxious Maisie asked, "Then where will the babies be born?"

"Here!" Pete snapped.

"There!" his mother responded at the same time.

Liz pushed back her chair and stood. "Please excuse me, Maisie, but I have lost my appetite."

Though everyone at the table protested, Liz slipped from the room and ran up the stairs, hoping she made her bathroom before what little she'd eaten made another appearance.

PETE ROSE to follow Beth but was forestalled by the arrival of Dansky.

"Good evening. I apologize for arriving in the middle of the evening meal," the man said politely, giving a half bow.

Maisie jumped up. "Not at all. Sit down beside Mr. Petrocelli and I'll fetch you a plate and silverware. There's more than enough food. 'Specially since Beth has lost her appetite," she added with a glare at Pete.

"I'm not the one who brought up the subject of babies." Pete seemed determined not to be colored the villain.

"You certainly weren't being considerate with Beth," Lady Hereford challenged. "Why, she must think you don't want to marry her."

"Beth knows exactly what I want, Mother. As I said earlier, we both recognize there are difficulties with our…marriage. Pressure from others doesn't relieve the situation."

"Have I missed something?" Dansky asked Petrocelli. "Have we had a crisis while I was away?"

"A tabloid reporter and his photographer sneaked onto the ranch and took at least one picture," Petrocelli said.

"That is the reason for the difficulties?" Dansky shook his head in confusion.

"No!" Pete snapped. "That's not the problem. In

fact, my mother sees the picture as a benefit, advertising our marriage. The only difficulty is that Beth won't commit to the marriage until I talk with her father!'' She wouldn't commit to anything, and that irritated Pete more than he'd believed possible.

''Then why don't we call him?'' Lady Hereford asked, the wide smile on her face telling them she believed she'd found the solution to the problem.

''No!'' both Dansky and Petrocelli said.

Pete looked at the two of them and then turned back to his mother. ''Beth says her father doesn't like to discuss serious issues over the phone.''

''It is true, my lady,'' Dansky hurriedly agreed. ''His Highness prefers to hold discussions in person.''

''Well, of course, so do I, but I can assure you His Highness needs to know of the problems we're encountering. He's busily making plans.''

Pete continued to watch the two men as they exchanged glances, fear in their eyes. Why were they so frightened by the idea of a phone call? ''Gentlemen?''

''I beg your lordship not to consider such action. Allow several more days' grace for you and the princess to...to talk about the difficulties. Surely something can be worked out.'' Dansky stared at Pete, waiting for his answer, as if his life hung in the balance.

Finally with a sigh Pete agreed. ''I don't think it will change anything, but I did originally agree to a week's visit. I don't suppose that much time will matter.'' Besides, he might lose Beth completely if the king was unreasonable. He needed these next few days to come to terms with his feelings for Beth.

The two men sighed and relaxed in their chairs. His mother wasn't as happy.

"I think you should call the king, Peter. He's a reasonable man."

"I'll talk to him, Mother, but not right now."

"Whenever you talk to him," Maisie muttered, "be sure and tell him about those babies."

LIZ LAY CURLED UP in a ball on the big bed, trying to control the shivers that shook her after losing her dinner. It was ridiculous to let the argument upset her. After all, they weren't arguing about her.

But that was the difficulty. She'd become the princess in her own head, because she'd fallen in love with the princess's man.

Of all the idiotic things to happen!

Suddenly the thought of going home to her mother and losing herself in her motherly embrace seemed like heaven. But she couldn't leave without some assistance, and she would be reneging on her contract, too.

Instead, she reached for the phone, the next best thing to being there, as the telephone companies said. She hoped by placing the call collect there would be no record of it on Pete's bill.

"Hello?"

"Mom? How are you? I'm sorry to call collect, but—"

"Don't be silly, child. That's no problem now. I

can't believe what a relief it is to be out of debt, all thanks to you. Where are you?''

''I...I'm still working. I won't be free until the weekend.''

''Can you tell me when you'll be here? I can't wait.''

''No, Mom, I can't. Things have gotten a little complicated.''

''Elizabeth Ann, are you in trouble?'' The concern in her mother's voice was like a balm to her wounds.

''Oh, Mom. How did you know?''

'''Cause you sound like you did that night you and your friends were in a car wreck.''

She'd been a teenager then, naive and sheltered. A phone call to her parents had solved most of her difficulties. Liz wished that same magic would work now.

''It's not the same. I'm safe—at least, physically— but I have some problems.''

''I wish I could help you. Are you sure you can't come home now?''

''No, Mom. I have to stay and do my job.'' Otherwise her mother wouldn't be out of debt and sound so happy. As happy as she'd ever sounded since her husband's death. Surely Liz could make it a few more days, for her mother's sake.

''Tell me about the problems.''

''I can't, Mom. I need to—''

A knock on her door caused her to sit bolt upright in the bed and drop the receiver. Immediately she snatched it up and whispered, ''I have to go, Mom. I'll call you later.''

She hung up without waiting for her mother's response, then called out, "Just a minute."

Running into the bathroom, she ran a comb through her hair and scrubbed tear tracks from her cheeks. Then she hurried to the door.

"Who is it?"

"It's me, with some dinner for you." Pete's voice was distinctive. She knew she'd recognize it for the rest of her life.

Easing the door open only a few inches, she stared up at his stern visage. "I'm not really hungry."

"You look pale. Did you throw up?"

She should've known he'd make her feel inelegant. "My stomach was uneasy. Perhaps I'm catching the flu."

"Nope. I think you're catching an aversion to arguments about the two of us." He pushed against the door. "Let me in, Beth. You need to eat something before you pass out again."

Maybe the talk with her mother had done her some good, because to her surprise, the food looked appetizing—except for the glass of wine Pete had thoughtfully included. She'd have much preferred a glass of milk.

"I'll take the tray, thank you," she said.

"Afraid to let me into the room? Afraid I'll throw you on the bed and have my way with you?"

How she wished he would. Then she could assuage her conscience by saying it wasn't her fault. But she knew he would never take her against her will. And her will knew it would be a terrible mistake. "No. I'm not afraid of that."

"Maybe you should be," he said with a rueful grin.

She couldn't refuse to let him enter now. Moving back from the door to let him carry in the tray, she indulged in a moment of true hunger as her gaze traveled up and down him. When he set the tray down on the coffee table and turned to her, she immediately lowered her lashes.

"Come sit down and eat," he ordered.

She sat on the sofa next to the coffee table, and he circled the sofa to sit beside her. He apparently intended to keep her company while she ate.

"Is your mother angry?" she asked before beginning to eat.

"No. I think she's a little perturbed with me, but not you. She thinks I'm being unreasonable."

Liz relaxed slightly, glad she hadn't drawn the dowager duchess's ire. Picking up the fork, she took a bite of broccoli.

Pete stared at her intently, as if he knew her secret.

He couldn't have overheard her, could he? After all, the princess didn't have a mother. She held her breath, wondering what was coming.

"So, who were you talking to?"

Chapter Ten

Liz heaved a big sigh and closed her eyes. She was going to have to stop underestimating this cowboy.

When she opened her eyes and lifted her gaze to him, he had one eyebrow raised and a questioning look on his face.

"I called a friend long-distance, but it was a collect call. You won't have to pay for it."

"A friend? I didn't know you had any friends."

She gasped. "You think I was hatched from an egg? That I'm so cold-blooded I can't make friends? You must not have a very high opinion of me."

"That's not what I meant!" he protested, and stretched out a hand toward her.

She leaned away. "It certainly sounded that way."

"I meant, I didn't know you had any friends here."

"I told you it was long-distance."

"Europe?" he asked, his eyebrow arching again. "You called Europe? What time is it there? One or two in the morning? Must've been a real good friend."

Raising her chin, Liz stared him down. "The best."

"Male?"

The flicker of jealousy she thought she saw in his eyes pleased her——until she remembered she'd vowed to keep her distance from him. "That is none of your business."

He rose from his chair, a frown on his face. "I guess it was male, since you won't say. And as your fiancé, I think it *is* my business."

"You're not my fiancé," she muttered, refusing to look at him.

"The hell I'm not! Why do you think my mother's here? Because she wants to see a real princess?" he asked scornfully. "She can do that any day of the week in England."

Her gaze traveled up his powerful form, noting his clenched fists on his hips, his traditional stance when he was irritated. With a sigh she pleaded, "Pete, can't you be reasonable?"

"Why should I be? You're refusing our engagement, putting me off, keeping your distance, pretending nothing was agreed upon." He took a turn about the room. "You're in Montana now. We're straight shooters around here. And that's what I expect from you."

She stood. "And what about what I expect from you?"

Her words apparently took him by surprise.

"What are you talking about?"

"I'm the future ruler of my country, but you refuse to acknowledge the importance of my role or my responsibility to my father and my country. You think you and your ranch are more important. Yet you want me to say our marriage will be great.'' She turned away and crossed her arms over her chest. "I can't do that.''

He moved to stand in front of her. "I think we can work things out.''

"How?''

"Maybe if we take the next couple of days to get…closer to each other, together we can—''

"This is all about me refusing to sleep with you, isn't it?'' Liz demanded. Stepping closer, she drilled him in the chest with one finger. "I'm right, aren't I? Your pride is hurt.''

"No! I admit I don't understand why you refuse me when you haven't refused anyone else this century, but that's not the problem!''

"I think—''

The door was thrown open. "Darlings!'' a beaming dowager duchess trilled. "I'm here to present my fait accompli.''

Liz froze, stunned by the woman's entrance.

Pete seemed to take it in stride. "What are you talking about, Mother?''

"I have accomplished the impossible. Dansky and Petrocelli have agreed you two should have the rest of the evening alone!''

She stood waiting for them to express their gratitude.

PETE REALLY WAS GRATEFUL to his mother for the chance to spend some time with Beth without those guards hovering. But he had to be careful with his princess. She wasn't in a grateful mood.

He peeked at her from the corner of his eye as he drove. She was staring rigidly out the window on the other side of the pickup, pressed against the door to put as much space between them as possible.

"I think you'll like the Melodrama."

She gave a slight sniff but didn't look at him.

"Aw, come on, Beth, give me a break. I didn't ask my mother to arrange some privacy for us. And I promised you I'd keep my distance."

No response.

"Any more distance between us and I'd be driving from the back," he muttered in exasperation.

He was encouraged by the tiny twitch of her lips. "Won't you at least speak to me?"

"Of course I will—as soon as I have something to say."

"You're not going to embarrass me in front of my friends, are you? A lot of them work at the Melodrama."

"They do?"

"Sure. This is something the community does for charity every summer. All the proceeds go to help people, and it brings in the tourists, too, which helps the economy."

As she relaxed her rigidity somewhat, he breathed easier. If he could keep the conversation off their personal problems for a while, she might even smile at him.

"So why don't you work there?"

"I have. I was the villain one summer, twirling my mustache and leering at all the women."

"That wasn't much of a stretch," she said politely, as if complimenting him.

"Hey! Low blow!"

Ah, there was her smile.

"I know."

He shrugged. "If it makes you feel better, I'll even endure cheap shots."

She turned more toward him. "Please don't be a martyr for me."

In spite of his progress, he couldn't let the moment pass. "I'd even do that for you, Beth, if it would resolve our problems."

Her face froze and he thought he'd lost all the ground he'd gained. Instead, after licking her lips, making him hunger for them beyond belief, she said softly, "Tonight let's pretend there's no problem. Let's just be friends, Pete, okay?"

He studied her pleading gaze before lifting her hand and bringing it to his lips. "Good friends?" he negotiated, grinning at her.

"Any kind of friend you want," she promised, "as long as the emphasis is on friend."

It wasn't what he wanted, but it sure as hell beat the war that had been going on. He kissed her hand again. "You've got a deal."

SEVERAL HOURS LATER Liz sat relaxed at a table at the Short Limb Saloon. Pete had taken her there after the show to join several couples. He'd told her that the bar was named after the Long Branch Saloon on an old television show. And she had to pretend she didn't remember Marshal Dillon and Dodge City.

Introducing her simply as his friend Beth, he'd left the table to go get them some drinks.

"So, Beth, are you from around here?" a blonde woman asked. Her name was Ann and she was with the man Pete had introduced as Larry, an old college friend.

"No, I'm not." She smiled and asked a question of her own. "Are you?"

"I'm actually from Helena, but Larry is a teacher and coach, and he comes out here to direct the Melodrama every summer. So I come with him of course."

"You did a marvelous job, Larry," Liz said, smiling at the man. "I laughed all the way through it."

"Yeah, I bet you did. Probably even when the villain's mustache slipped down to his chin."

The other woman at the table, a petite brunette who was part Native American, grinned. "You have to admit, Larry, it did spice up that slow scene."

"Hey, I told you it isn't slow, it's stately."

Apparently Liz had stumbled into an ongoing argument, because the brunette and Larry launched into a debate that seemed well-rehearsed. Liz didn't mind, as long as it kept questions at bay.

It had been the same during the show. She hadn't realized how much tension she'd been holding in until the lights went out and she could watch the play without fear of being discovered as a fraud. She'd held Pete's hand and shared the laughter with him, feeling about ten years younger.

Pete and the brunette's husband returned to the table, a tray of drinks and a bowl of popcorn in their hands.

"Did you meet everyone, sweetheart?" Pete asked, kissing her on the cheek as he sat down.

His action was hardly a demonstration of undying devotion, but it sent a charge of electricity around the table, drawing all eyes to Liz.

She wanted to strangle him.

"You got an announcement to make?" Larry asked.

"About what?" Pete asked. "The play? It was the best ever, Larry. We laughed so hard—"

"No, about 'sweetheart' here." The others nodded to second Larry's words and gesture toward Liz.

Shocked, Liz stared first at Larry and then Pete. "What does he mean?"

Blood crept up Pete's cheeks. "Come on, Larry, knock it off."

"Well, hell, Pete, the last time you called a woman sweetheart—that blonde, remember?—you almost married her."

Suddenly Liz understood Pete's friends' reactions. She'd assumed he always threw around endearments when he was with a woman. Apparently that wasn't the case.

"We're just friends," she hurriedly said, then hoping to head off any explanations, asked, "How long have you been married, Larry?"

"Too long," he replied with a nudge and a grin directed at his wife.

"And you? I'm sorry, I don't know your name,"

she said to the other man who'd helped Pete carry the drinks.

"Sorry, I'm Bart and this is Mavis, my wife. We've been married almost ten years now. She trapped me in kindergarten."

Everyone laughed as Mavis dug her elbow into Bart's ribs. Meanwhile Liz was trying to think of other questions to direct the conversation. "Mavis, I recognize you as the heroine in the play. Do you work in it, too, Bart?"

"Yeah," he drawled. "I'm the best boy."

"Beth probably doesn't understand that term. She's from Europe." Pete's statement immediately undid all Liz's work, drawing the conversation right back to her.

She grabbed the glass Pete had put in front of her and blindly took a swallow, only to discover he'd brought her white wine.

"From Europe? What are you doing here?" Ann asked. "Are you an old friend of Pete's from England? You don't sound English, though I do hear a slight accent, now that you mention it."

"No, I'm not from England, though it's a lovely country. Have you ever been there?"

The two couples shook their heads simultaneously and continued to stare at her.

"It's quite different from America, especially Los Angeles. I just arrived from L.A. Everything is so peaceful here compared to that madhouse."

Fortunately Larry, who seemed to be the most gregarious of the foursome, couldn't resist comparing his beloved home with the wicked city of Los Angeles.

Liz got several safe minutes from his ramblings. She sneaked a look at her watch, hoping she could convince Pete to end the evening soon.

Larry's wife interrupted him with another question for Liz. "What were you doing in L.A.?"

"Just stopping over. Have you ever been to see the famous handprints in the sidewalk?"

"You mean the ones outside that Chinese theater?" Bart asked.

Liz nodded, and the man took up that subject with a funny story about a childhood visit. Several others added to the conversation with childhood remembrances and Liz relaxed again.

Until Phyllis, the woman from the store where she'd purchased her jeans, passed by. She nodded to everyone and Liz thought the woman was going to continue on her way. Instead, she stopped and turned to Liz.

"Why, Princess, I didn't see you for a minute. I thought you'd already left town."

"No," Liz said softly, "I'm still here."

"Be sure you come see me before you leave." She waved and walked off.

Mavis asked, her eyes wide. "Princess? You're a princess?"

The other three leaned toward Liz as if she was about to reveal a state secret.

PETE OPENED the truck door for Beth an hour later, a grin on his face.

Of course he was happy. He'd just proved to himself again that Beth was perfect for life here in Montana. She didn't want the fame and notoriety that went with the lifestyle of a princess. Just like him.

Before she'd arrived at the ranch, he'd been sure she'd take one look at its isolation and everyday life and say a quick goodbye. Not only had she stayed, she'd avoided all formality and hadn't demanded any special attention.

Tonight she'd done everything she could to keep the conversation off her. Until Phyllis made it impossible. His friends weren't unsophisticated hicks, but even they had been fascinated with a real live princess.

"Thanks for pointing out to my friends that I hold a title, too," he said, grinning as he climbed into the truck.

"Why should I suffer alone?" she said.

"You know, if you gave up your title and settled down here, you wouldn't have to suffer."

The darkness seemed to swallow her up—or maybe it was her silence. Finally she said, "I can't do that."

He started the engine and backed out of the parking place. "I know."

But he wished she could. For the first time ever he'd found a woman who fit perfectly into his life and drew him to her like no woman before.

But like a lot of Mother Nature's jokes on the human race, she came with a catch. She could be his about fifty percent of the time—and belong to Cargenia the rest of her days.

"I don't like the idea of a part-time marriage." He regretted the words as soon as they escaped his mouth.

"Friends, Pete. We're pretending to be friends, remember?" she said softly.

He gave a bitter laugh. "That little act didn't fool my friends, did it?"

"Nope. But how was I to know you don't go around calling other women sweet names? I figured you had a Romeo reputation."

"Like you?"

"That's the second time tonight you've made a comment about my social reputation, mister. I'm getting tired of it."

"You sounded almost like Annie Oakley asking me to get out of Dodge," he said, chuckling. "You'll shock a few people when you return to Cargenia."

A tense silence filled the truck and he tried to see her face in the darkness. "Did I offend you?"

"Which time?" she demanded crisply. "When you implied I'd slept with anyone who asked me this century? Or likening me to Romeo?"

"Hell, Beth, I didn't mean that earlier remark. I was frustrated. And I don't handle that particular emotion well."

"No kidding," she said.

"Damn, another week, and no one will ever guess you're from Europe."

"I...I was only imitating you."

"Don't let those two escorts of yours hear you or they'll blame me."

"I wonder how your mother convinced them to leave us alone?"

There was a breathless quality to her voice that aroused him. It made him think of a dark room, a big bed and the two of them pressed together, nothing coming between them. He cleared his throat. "I don't know."

"Does your mother ride?"

"Of course she does. Mother was quite a horse-woman in her youth. She rides with an English saddle, but when she comes home, she reverts."

"Perhaps we'll all go for a ride tomorrow."

"Looking for escorts? Already had your fill of me alone?" He reached over and picked up her hand. It felt cold and small in his.

"No, of course not. But…but it might be better that way. We both know what happens if we're alone too much."

"I've behaved tonight!" he protested. He ought to get credit for his abstinence since he was suffering through it.

"The night's not over," she reminded him.

"I can control myself."

"I'm not sure I can."

He wondered if he'd only imagined her response because he wanted her so badly. "Would you repeat that?" he asked.

He felt rather than saw her shake her head. Squeezing her hand, he said, "I thought you said you weren't sure you could control yourself where I'm concerned."

"Pete, I never blamed you…entirely, for what has happened. But just because you're sexy and willing doesn't mean we should…do something we'll regret."

"I don't know who you think is going to regret it. It's sure not me."

"You could be wrong."

Her soft answer filled the cab of the truck as he drove. Neither spoke again until he stopped the truck beside the house.

When he didn't make any move to get out, Beth stirred. "Thanks for a few hours when I could forget all the arguing and questions. I had a lot of fun."

"Me, too. My friends liked you, in spite of your being a princess."

"Just like they like you, in spite of your being the second son of a duke."

He grinned. "They don't even remember that—unless someone reminds them." But he wasn't angry with her for bringing up his past. In a way it gave them one more thing in common.

And there were many. The laughter they'd shared tonight had been so much richer because she was beside him. He'd seen that stupid Melodrama so many times he could recite every line of it. Yet tonight the same story had seemed fresh and original.

Beth made everything around her seem new and exciting. The thought of her leaving, however, chased the sunlight away. To his surprise he was even considering surrendering to the terms of her life in Cargenia if he could have her with him part of the year.

"Can we continue as friends the next few days until I leave?" she whispered.

Her question jerked him out of his thoughts.

"I'll try, Beth. But it's hard."

"I know."

They got out of the truck, but neither moved toward the house, both reluctant to reenter the real world.

Suddenly the back door burst open. "Darlings! I'm so glad you're back. Guess who's on the phone? Hurry, I told him you'd be right in." His mother's form was silhouetted against the kitchen light that spilled out onto the back porch.

Pete felt Beth's death grip on his shirt. Her body began trembling like an aspen in the wind. What was going on here?

"Beth, dear, come along," Lady Hereford called out. "It's your father."

Chapter Eleven

For a moment Liz sagged against Pete's strong body. Her father. How she wished her real father was waiting to talk to her. But instead, a king was waiting to communicate with his daughter.

Dear heaven, she didn't even know what the princess called her father. She needed help. Fast.

"Where are Dansky and Petrocelli?" she asked as she reluctantly withdrew from Pete's protective embrace.

"They're talking to your father now, dear," his mother said.

Liz stepped toward Lady Hereford only to be stopped by Pete. She looked up at him questioningly.

"Are you all right?" he asked, staring at her. "You have red splotches on your face."

The wine! She'd forgotten about its effect on her. She tried to keep her smile steady. "Of course." She covered her face with her hands. "When I get tired, my skin, uh, reddens. I mustn't keep my father waiting."

Another lie for the princess to deal with. She

crossed to the porch and moved past Pete's mother. In the kitchen Maisie pointed her down the hall, indicating that her escorts were in Pete's office.

Opening the door, she slipped into the room to discover Dansky on the phone, with Petrocelli standing nearby looking anxious. She crossed to his side and whispered, "What do I call my father?"

"In front of others 'Your Highness,'" he whispered in return. "Alone, you always call him Papa. Remember to say as little as possible."

"Why did he call?"

"He didn't. Lady Hereford decided to call him after she tricked us into agreeing to your night out. Did anything go wrong?"

"No, other than meeting a number of people who now know the princess is visiting. And drinking wine. I'm allergic to it." Then, with a searching glance at Petrocelli, she added, "I had fun."

He frowned. "That is good, but now you must deal with the king. Be careful." He gave her a little nudge toward Dansky, who was holding out the phone.

"Papa?" she said softly.

"My daughter, I am proud of you. I understand you have charmed the cowboy. Good. I have invited him and his mother to come visit next month when we will finalize the agreement. Continue to charm him. It is understood?"

"Yes, Papa."

"Good. Let me talk to Dansky."

She handed over the receiver with a sigh of relief, then realized all her worry was for naught. She'd only had to speak three words. The man asked no questions about his daughter's well-being. Only about the status of the marriage agreement.

Once more she felt sympathy for the princess. Liz's father might be dead, but at least she had wonderful memories of time spent with him, of his concern and love. The poor princess was a tool her father used for his and his country's well-being. Not a daughter he loved and cherished.

As if he'd read her mind, Petrocelli muttered, "He does care about her, but the marriage is very important to him. If this marriage fell through, he would arrange for another to a less attractive man. You are truly helping the princess, miss."

Yes, but am I helping Pete? That question bothered Liz the most. And not just because she loved him herself. Even if she never saw him again, she wanted him to be happy. "Will the princess be content here half the year? Will she want to have a family?"

"She will not stay here that long. She bores easily and moves about, traveling a lot. But she will have an heir of course. It is her duty."

They both fell silent as Dansky hung up the phone, waiting for him to speak.

"You did well," he announced to Liz, beaming at her. "The king is most pleased with our work." He looked at Petrocelli. "He has promised us a large bonus if the marriage is arranged."

Petrocelli didn't seem impressed with his friend's words. "I would not count on a reward just yet. Once the princess and Pete are together, I believe he will realize she will not be happy on the ranch."

Dansky began pacing the floor. "We will warn her

to pretend an interest until after the marriage ceremony. Because of Miss Caine's performance, he will believe her to be sincere for a short while.''

''No!'' Liz protested. ''You must encourage the princess to be honest with him. Petrocelli, don't you see? You will only make both of them miserable if they marry under false pretenses.'' She pleaded with her eyes, as well as her words.

There was hesitation on Petrocelli's face, but Dansky overrode any response he might make.

''Nonsense! I told you before this is a business arrangement. Emotions have no place in such a marriage.''

''How can you say that?'' She wanted to scream at the top of her lungs, to slug the man for his patronizing words as he stared down his nose at her.

''You simply do not understand that Lord Peter, too, will gain by the marriage. He will be a prince and one day a king. And I believe there are monetary concerns, also.''

She knew that. But Liz remembered the man who'd held her in his arms, protected her from the reporters, carried her because he thought she was sick. Pete led with his heart, not his wallet. All the acreage in Montana wouldn't make up for the betrayal they were perpetrating.

She felt sick at heart.

There was a knock on the door.

Petrocelli opened it and Pete stood in the hallway. ''Is the king still on the phone?''

''No, the conversation just ended,'' Dansky informed him. ''The king is most satisfied with...your hospitality. He looks forward to returning it next month.''

"Next month?'' Pete asked, a puzzled look on his face.

"Yes. He extended an invitation to you and Lady Hereford to visit.''

"July is a busy month on the ranch. I was thinking I'd return with Beth. I can spare a week now.''

"You must discuss the timing with your mother of course, Pete, but the king has a busy schedule," Petrocelli warned. "He would not be able to spend much time with you if you change the visit at such a late date.''

Pete grinned at Liz and she couldn't hold back a smile in response. "Good. I don't want to spend a lot of time with the king. I prefer to visit with the princess.''

"The princess also has many official duties.''

Liz could tell Pete was becoming irritated with the men's warnings. He glared at Dansky. "Maybe she'll have to make some changes.''

The two men gasped as if he'd delivered a slap on the face with his glove.

"My lord,'' Dansky protested, "surely you understand fulfilling one's duties. After all, you are a blue blood yourself.''

"But I'm not chained to silly rituals. I work for a living." He turned to Liz. "And I'm getting damn tired of having to follow someone else's rules.''

She wanted to tell him to take the opportunity to run as fast as he could from the marriage agreement.

But she couldn't. Shrugging, she said, "I have no choice."

Before he could answer, as he surely intended to do, his mother appeared behind him. "Did you have a delightful visit with your father, Beth, dear?"

Liz nodded but said nothing as the woman continued, "I'm so looking forward to visiting your country. And soon to be Peter's country, also. To think, my son will one day be king." She sighed, then hurriedly added, "Not that I'm hoping for your father's death, my dear. No, of course not."

"Mother," Pete said with irritation in his voice, "I wanted to go to Cargenia when Beth returns, not in July. We're busy at the ranch in July. I need to be here that entire month."

"Darling boy, you are too ridiculous. Surely your marriage must take precedence over some stupid cows." She smiled at Liz. "What will your fiancée think?"

"I've been informed by Beth that we are not engaged," he said, shooting a cool look her way.

Liz knew he'd made the remark to annoy her, but it was his mother who rose to the challenge.

"What? Whatever are you talking about, child? Of course you are engaged. The king and I came to an agreement three months ago."

"Only if I approved, Mother. Remember? That was the reason for Beth's visit—for me to approve the match. *Then* the papers would be signed."

His mother cocked one eyebrow at him, much in his own style, and said, "Are you telling me you oppose the match? Don't be ridiculous. I've seen the way you look at each other." She chuckled, her eyes dancing.

Liz decided it was time to intervene before Lady Hereford said something that would really embarrass her and Pete. "Lady Hereford, Pete and I have enjoyed getting to know each other, but there are difficulties to work out. Until the papers are signed, I don't consider either of us to be committed to the marriage."

"Oh, fiddle! Of course you will marry."

Liz gave up the argument. "Well, since everything is settled, I hope you'll excuse me. I need to rest, for I hope to join you in a ride tomorrow."

"That's probably a good idea. Your face is turning redder," Pete said, staring at her, turning everyone else's gaze to her face, too.

Liz smothered a groan. She'd only had a small sip of the wine. Just once couldn't her skin have cooperated?

"Is something the matter, Your Highness?" Petrocelli immediately asked.

"I am tired. My skin reddens if I do not get enough rest." Before anyone else could comment on her deficiency, Liz slipped from the room and ran for the stairs. She wanted no more comments on her skin. And she wanted no more debates on a future that didn't include her.

AFTER A RESTLESS NIGHT Pete was out early the next morning astride Diamond, his favorite mount, enjoying a Montana summer morning—and facing his demons.

If he gave in to the emotions Beth evoked, his life would be changed forever. He would spend a lot less time here at the home he loved. The compensation would be the time he spent with Beth. But even then, he would have to share her with her countrymen.

If he resisted those feelings, turned his back on Beth and her father, he would lose the ranch possibly, and he would be alone. For the rest of his life, as far as he could tell.

Because Beth had touched him as no other woman ever had.

An hour later, when he turned his horse back toward the house, he hadn't come to any conclusions—except he wished Beth wasn't a princess.

He dismounted in front of the barn and shouted for Joseph. The old man came out of the barn.

"There you be. Maisie's lookin' for you."

"Why?"

"She don't tell me nothin', boy. Just skedaddle on up to the house. She'll tell you."

"Okay. Take care of my horse for me, would you?"

Pete strode to the house, wondering what problem Maisie had called about. It was becoming difficult to even remember problems on the ranch, for Beth was now the center of his thoughts.

"Maisie?" he called as he stepped into the kitchen.

She turned from the stove to put her hands on her waist. "Mary called from the grocery store. They got in their early shipment of them newspapers. The ones with that picture in it."

He'd almost forgotten about the photographer and reporter trespassing on his land. "Damn!"

"What's wrong?"

He spun around to find Beth standing in the doorway, watching him. "That picture has surfaced."

"The one of us? Is it in the paper?"

"Yeah. One of those tabloids. Maisie, call the bunkhouse and tell Harvey to go into town and buy up all the copies."

Maisie went to the phone to do as he asked.

"You can't buy all the copies in the world," Beth whispered, still watching him.

"Nope," he agreed, stepping to her side and wrapping his arms around her. "But I can buy all the ones in Parsons, Montana. Maybe the picture was unfocused, anyway."

"Maybe."

When he tilted her chin up so his lips could cover hers, she didn't protest. In fact, he thought she was as eager for their kiss as he. When he finally lifted his head, he said, "That's to make up for the goodnight kiss I didn't get last night."

"Oh. I thought it was your good-morning kiss."

He smiled. "Nope. That's coming next."

Her arms went around his neck as their lips met. The kiss made him forget the picture, the ranch, Cargenia and everything else. Only Beth ruled his thoughts—and his body.

"Here now, you two cut that out. You haven't even had breakfast yet," Maisie protested.

Pete slowly released Beth, but his gaze remained on her flushed face, a smile on his lips. She was beautiful, with her dark hair tousled, her eyes sparkling. Only Maisie's presence kept him from reaching for Beth again.

"You ready for breakfast, boss, or are you gonna shower first?" Maisie asked.

"I'd better shower. Want to scrub my back?" he asked Beth, a teasing grin on his lips.

"I'd love to," she tossed back, "but I just did my nails. I wouldn't want to smudge them."

The flirtatious look on her face almost made him throw her over his shoulder, smudged nails and all, and run up the stairs. "Careful, little lady, or you'll find yourself in the shower whether you want to be or not."

Beth scooted across the room to Maisie's side. "Maisie will protect me."

"I doubt it. Maisie wants some babies around here."

"Pete!" Beth said with a gasp and red cheeks.

"Pete!" Maisie protested at the same time. "I wouldn't be wantin' any babies without a weddin' first."

"Oh, yeah, I forgot. And we can't be talking about a wedding until we sign some papers. Right, Beth?"

"Right," she said faintly.

"Keep my breakfast warm, Maisie," Pete ordered, and headed for the stairs. Suddenly all the humor had gone out of the conversation.

AN HOUR LATER the entire household was lounging around the breakfast table, enjoying second or third cups of coffee, when a truck was heard lumbering down the drive.

"That should be Harvey," Maisie said from where she stood at the sink.

Pete rose to his feet. "I'll go get the papers."

"This is like waiting for the reviews after opening night at the theater," Lady Hereford said cheerfully.

Liz stared at the woman, wondering how she could compare their situation to such a social event. Liz herself was not looking forward to seeing the picture. She only hoped no one, in particular the king, realized it wasn't the princess.

No conversation interrupted the tense silence while Pete was gone. Lady Hereford, buttering another biscuit, was the only one unaffected.

With a stern face Pete stepped into the kitchen, a pile of papers in his arms. He set them in his chair and handed the top one to Liz. His face had already told her what she wanted to know. The picture wasn't one she'd want published.

Unfolding the paper, she discovered their picture rated the front page. It showed exactly what she remembered. A lot of heat. She was buried in Pete's embrace, leaving her face barely visible. She didn't think anyone would know she wasn't the princess.

Just in case anyone doubted their identities, separate pictures of the princess and Lord Peter were alongside the larger picture. Petrocelli gave her a covert nod, indicating he believed they were safe, also.

"Wonderful!" Lady Hereford exclaimed as she examined the evidence. "Everyone will believe your marriage is a real romance. Your father will be most pleased, Beth.''

Liz looked at Dansky and Petrocelli again. Both were intent on the article accompanying the picture.

''Why is everyone looking so gloomy?'' Lady Hereford demanded. ''This picture is perfect. You couldn't have planned it better.''

''But we didn't plan it, Mother,'' Pete said. ''In fact, they invaded our privacy. I'm going to talk to my attorney.''

Petrocelli lifted his head and said, ''They repeated every piece of gossip ever written about the princess.''

Pete's frown grew deeper.

''And about you, Pete,'' Dansky added.

Liz's interest increased and she picked up the paper again. ''I didn't know there was gossip about Pete.''

He cleared his throat and tried to take her copy of the paper away from her. ''I don't think you should read that. Everything printed isn't the truth.''

Her eyebrows soared. ''Oh, really?''

Pete understood Liz's meaning and his cheeks flushed. ''Point taken.''

Liz rewarded him with a smile before turning her attention to what was written. It didn't take her long to understand why Pete had made remarks about her past behavior. According to the article, the princess had slept with every titled man in Europe and a few pretenders, too.

In Pete's case, they listed every romance he'd had since high school. There was even a picture of a blonde he'd been engaged to after college. Liz figured she was the one his friend had referred to the night before.

Before they finished reading, the phone rang. Maisie, reading over Lady Hereford's shoulder, moved to the phone. Then she said, "Pete, it's the local paper, wanting confirmation that you're gettin' married."

"Tell them no comment."

"Pete! No! Of course you must confirm it. You want all the publicity you can get," his mother insisted.

Maisie repeated Pete's order. Hanging up the phone, she turned back toward the table, but before she could take even a step, the phone rang again.

When she faced Pete this time, holding the phone against her chest, she whispered, "It's the *New York Times*."

"Same answer," he said tersely. Again his mother protested, but he ignored her.

"But, darling, why won't you tell them you are to be married? It will please the king so much."

"Because I'm not sure it will please me," Pete growled. "Or Beth, since she won't even say we're engaged."

The phone rang again, another newspaper wanting confirmation of the story. As Maisie dealt with each caller, everyone around the table grew more irritated. Pete finally bolted for the barn, telling his mother and Liz to join him when they were ready to ride.

Maisie was muttering something under her breath about not getting any work done, and Liz offered to answer the phone for a while. "I can say no comment as well as you, Maisie. I'll go to Pete's office and you can turn the ringer off on this phone.''

With Maisie's grateful agreement, Liz spent the next hour saying no comment. Her escorts retreated to their rooms for a period of time before they, accompanied by Lady Hereford, joined Liz in Pete's office.

''When do you and Lady Hereford plan to go for a ride?'' Dansky asked.

''Is ten o'clock all right with you, my lady?'' Liz asked politely.

''I suppose. But I do wish I could change your mind about announcing—''

The phone rang again.

After Liz finished offering the standard answer, she turned to Dansky. ''I suggest Petrocelli remain here and answer the phone for Maisie while you accompany us on our ride.''

Petrocelli nodded, a grateful smile on his face.

Dansky frowned but nodded in agreement.

The phone rang again and Liz answered, prepared to deliver her practiced answer.

''I demand to speak to Dansky at once.''

''I'm sorry, we have no comment,'' Liz said, even as she was surprised by the request for Dansky.

''I do not care what you say. I will speak with Dansky at once!''

Liz's eyes widened and her knees began shaking. Covering the receiver with her hand, she whispered to Petrocelli, ''Take Lady Hereford to the kitchen for...for another cup of coffee.''

He must have heard the urgency in her voice because, in spite of that lady's protests, the two of them left the room.

Liz held out the phone to Dansky. ''I think it's the real princess.''

Chapter Twelve

Pete opened the door to his office. "I thought you were coming for a ride," he said to Beth as she stood beside Dansky.

She jumped as if he'd shot her, her eyes wide.

"What's wrong?" he asked. "Did I scare you?"

"N-no. I was concentrating on... I was thinking about... Dansky and I were talking."

Narrowing his eyes, he studied her. "Dansky's on the phone."

"Yes, it just rang."

"Another newspaper wanting a quote?"

"No. A call for him."

"The king?" He couldn't think who else would be calling Dansky there at his ranch.

Beth only shook her head.

"Who is it?"

"I don't know. The person didn't give a name."

"No! You must not!" Dansky ordered sternly into the phone.

Beth looked like a bundle of nerves, Pete thought.

"Perhaps we'd better go to the kitchen," she suggested, "and give Dansky some privacy."

"Okay." He stood aside for her to precede him. As he followed her out into the hall after closing the office door, however, he caught her arm and pulled her to him, turning her around so he could steal a kiss. He could hardly stand to be in the same room with her without touching her at least once.

Though startled, Beth warmed to him at once. Her lips parted in invitation, her arms went around him and she snuggled against him. In no time his body was reacting to her, showing her his readiness to head for the stairs and the nearest bed rather than the kitchen.

She finally pulled away. "We'd better not do this. There might be more cameras."

"In the hallway?"

"Someone might open a door," she said, all the while keeping her gaze on his lips.

"Then quit looking at me that way."

"What way?"

"Like you want me to kiss you again." Scarcely before the words were out, his mouth was on hers. She opened to him, stretching up to accommodate his height, pressing more tightly against him. He forgot about the problems with their match, the changes loving her would require. He just knew he wanted Beth in his life.

The moment was cut short when the office door opened.

"Your Highness, I need to speak to you, please,"

Dansky ordered as if he'd interrupted a polite conversation, not a passionate embrace.

"Not now, Dansky, we're going riding," Pete said. He knew he would have to adjust to Beth's role as princess interfering with their privacy, but not now.

"Pete, I must see what Dansky wants before we go out. I'm sure it won't take long."

He knew he was being unreasonable, but Pete hated it when she chose her escorts' side over his. It made him feel she didn't really care about him. "No! I'm tired of—"

She covered his lips with her fingers. "I'll meet you at the barn in ten minutes. I have to put on my boots, anyway, so Dansky can talk to me while I do so."

He didn't bother trying to hide his anger. Stepping away from the body he'd just held and thought he'd never let go, he roared, "Fine!" and stomped toward the kitchen.

"Ask Petrocelli to join us, please," she called after him, as if her mind was totally absorbed with whatever problems Dansky had.

How could she have completely forgotten the moment they'd just shared?

LIZ ALREADY HAD one boot on by the time Petrocelli joined her and Dansky in her bedroom. Dansky was pacing the floor, unwilling to speak before his partner arrived.

"What is the matter?" Petrocelli, slightly out of breath, asked.

"The princess called," Dansky said in a low voice,

drawing nearer to Liz. "She was angered by the picture." He turned to glare at her. "The princess feels you have betrayed her."

"Me?" Liz squeaked in surprise. She'd never considered— Well, maybe she had realized the princess wouldn't want her to consort with her future husband. "Then she shouldn't have sent me in her place!"

"She did not understand that Pete would react in such a fashion to their marital agreement."

"But you went to L.A. and told her, didn't you?"

Dansky muttered, "Yes, but she wouldn't listen."

Petrocelli waved a hand, as if dismissing all the hurt feelings and arguments. "What did the princess say?"

"She intended to come here at once and denounce Miss Caine."

Dansky's statement stunned both Liz and Petrocelli.

"Come here?" Liz gasped.

"Denounce her? But doesn't she realize she will indict herself as part of the conspiracy?" Petrocelli asked, his voice rising.

"Shh!" Dansky warned, with a glance at the closed door. "No one must hear us!" He cleared his throat and continued in a low voice. "I explained the complexity of the situation, including the king's reaction, and she took a more moderate tone. I promised there would be no more such...events." He glared at Liz. "And she calmed down."

Liz wasn't appeased. "Well, I think she's got her nerve. She wants to have her cake and eat it, too, and that just doesn't happen."

"For a princess it does," Petrocelli said softly. "The princess may be spoiled, Miss Caine, but she orders the world the way she wants it."

"Does she? She has a father who is more concerned with selling her into marriage than with her happiness. She is pursued by the paparazzi all over the world. And her every move must be choreographed by the two of you. I think I prefer my independence."

Petrocelli shrugged. "There is a price to be paid for everything."

Silence fell among the three. Finally Liz broke it. "What do we do now?"

Petrocelli answered. "Continue as we have. Avoid any, uh, intimate situations with Pete. Make no commitments to Lady Hereford no matter how much she presses you. Today is Thursday and we are to leave on Saturday morning. Only forty-eight more hours. Can you do it?"

Liz drew a deep breath. Forty-eight more hours and then she'd never see Pete again. Forty-eight more hours of lies and deceit. Forty-eight more hours of paradise…and hell.

"Yes, of course. I think we'd better hurry to the barn, Dansky. Pete is already angry with us."

"Why is he angry?" Petrocelli asked.

"Because he thinks he should give the orders," Dansky muttered. "I needed to talk to her and he wanted her to go with him at once."

Liz pulled on her second boot and stood. Picking up her hat and gloves, she headed for the door without speaking to the two men. She had enough to deal with.

They followed her from the room, Petrocelli catching her elbow. "We know these last two days will be difficult for you," he whispered, "but please remember the importance of our job."

"Right," she muttered. It was the best she could do in the circumstances.

When she and Dansky reached the barn, Harvey was waiting for them with their mounts, but there was no sign of Pete or his mother.

"Pete and Mary Margaret went on ahead. He said to tell you that you could join them if'n you want." Harvey shot Liz a questioning look and then continued, "Just aim for that peak straight ahead and you'll run into them. They're heading for a pretty little lake just over a couple of hills."

"Thanks, Harvey. I'm afraid Pete got angry because I had to handle difficulties related to my country. We will quickly catch up with them."

Harvey grinned. "That Pete's a hardheaded one, isn't he? They took a picnic lunch with 'em from Maisie, so you'll be well fed."

"Wonderful."

Harvey assisted her into the saddle as he had before, and she and Dansky set off.

After a few minutes, Dansky spoke. "Lord Peter seems to be growing more difficult as our visit progresses."

"Yes. As I've said before, I'm afraid this marriage will be a disaster. He resents any time given to the ruling of Cargenia. That will cause difficulties in the future.'' She held her breath, wondering if she'd managed to convince Dansky to abort their plan.

"As long as those difficulties don't arise until after the wedding, we will have succeeded."

"Surely the idea of a fairy-tale wedding and marriage must be sustained beyond leaving the church for it to have any effect on the economy."

Dansky shrugged and guided his horse around a low-hanging branch. "The princess will make it appear they are happy until the first child is born."

Liz's heart clenched in pain and anger. *She* wanted to be the mother of Pete's children. But even more, she didn't want a child brought into the world when everyone, except Pete, knew the marriage was a disaster.

Unless, of course, Pete fell in love with the real princess.

Could she be big enough to hope for such a thing?

Liz urged her mount to a canter. "Come on, I want to catch up with Pete and his mother." And outrun such difficult questions.

"I DON'T SEE why we didn't wait for Beth and Dansky. I'm afraid they'll be offended by your behavior, Peter.''

"Mother, I'm offended by their behavior, so that'll make everything equal," Pete returned as he swung down from the saddle. They had reached one of his favorite places on the ranch, a small jewel of a lake in the foothills.

"Peter, if I didn't know better, I'd think you were trying to discourage the princess."

He gave a bark of laughter that surprised even him. How ironic that now, when he wanted to marry Beth, his mother would think that. Remembering the first day Beth had arrived at his ranch, he smiled even more. "I don't want to discourage Beth."

"No, I didn't think you did. You look at her the way your father looked at me." His mother's dreamy smile matched his.

"Do you miss him?"

She glanced at him sharply. "Of course I do!"

"Me, too."

She swung down from her horse with as much agility as ever. "He was a wonderful man. And his two sons are just like him," she added, hugging Pete.

"Not exactly. But we try."

"Then you should try to work out your difficulties with Beth. She's a lovely girl—much to my surprise."

He gave his mother a wry look. "Strange that you would promote a marriage with a woman you thought wasn't lovely."

"I'm only trying to do what I can for your future, Peter. Robert will have heirs. You will never be the duke."

"I hope not! Mother, is that what this is all about? Do you think I envy Robert the title?" He shook his head in amazement. How could his own mother misunderstand him so?

Lady Hereford moved to a flat rock and sat down. "Darling, I know you say it makes no difference to you now, but one day you will feel cheated because you didn't inherit the title. I don't want any dissension between the two of you.''

Pete let out relieved laughter. Finally he'd found the key to his mother's machinations. ''Mother, dear, Robert knows I don't envy him the title—or the responsibilities that go with it. I'm more than content here on the ranch. Or I would be if I knew you wouldn't sell it away from me.''

Her cheeks heated up, but she looked him right in the eye. ''Of course I wouldn't do such a thing. Your grandfather and I discussed the future of the ranch long before he died. I told him to leave it to you directly, but he thought I should be the heir.''

''But you said— Mother, you rat!''

''Forgive me,'' she said softly, extending her hand to him. ''I only wanted what was best for you.''

He embraced his mother, feeling closer to her than he had in years. ''I ought to wring your neck. You've caused more trouble than you know.''

''How?''

''I've fallen in love with Beth.'' It surprised him how good it felt to say those words. He hadn't admitted the truth before now.

Instead of looking upset, she beamed at him. ''How wonderful! Maisie and I thought you had, but I'm glad you realize it. Now everything will work out just fine.''

''Will it? My wife will be the future ruler of a small country in Europe and I'll be tied here to the ranch.''

''But, dear, if you don't want—''

''Of course I want the ranch. It's my home, my life. I never expected to fall for Beth. I thought... Oh, never mind. Now I'll have to spend a lot of time away from here. Or away from Beth. And our children won't think of the ranch as home. They'll probably stay in Cargenia most of the time. Especially the oldest. He'll be the next ruler.''

Pete turned away from his mother and stared across the lake, the fresh summer breeze ruffling his hair. He loved this ranch so much, and he'd always looked forward to one day passing that love on to his own child. The freedom he had, that he could give his child, seemed priceless compared to Beth's lifestyle.

But could he give up Beth? He'd been wrestling with that difficulty the past several days. With a sigh he faced his mother again. "I'll wait and go with you to Cargenia in July. The men will take care of things here. But I want your support in negotiating the amount of time Beth will have to be in Cargenia, at least until she assumes the throne. Will you back me?''

"Of course, my dear. I'm sure the king will be reasonable.''

"I wish I could be as sure. Because the thing that disturbs me most of all is Beth's willingness to go along with whatever her father wants.''

LIZ LET OUT a sigh of relief when they topped the second hill and saw a beautiful little lake spread out below them. Even better were the two people, along with their horses, at the edge of the lake.

"There they are,'' she said to Dansky.

"I am grateful. I'm afraid I haven't ridden this long

in several years. Don't forget to stiffen your posture now that they are in sight.''

Liz sighed. She'd enjoyed the ride, relaxed in the saddle, letting Beauty's steady gait eat up the distance. Now, however, she must resume her role of princess.

''At least you'll have a break before we head back. One of Maisie's picnics will be a great reward for your fortitude.'' She started her horse down the path, turning to smile at Dansky.

''I hope we will have time to enjoy it. There is a mass of clouds building in the west.''

Liz brought her head up and looked. Dansky was right. With all her worrying, she hadn't noticed the change. ''I think we'll have a couple of hours before it reaches us, but Pete will be better able to estimate it. In any case we'd better speed up.''

When they reached the lake, Pete was at her side before she could dismount, reaching for her waist and swinging her down from Beauty. ''Thank you,'' she said, smiling tentatively at him. She didn't know if he was still angry or not.

''Welcome,'' he murmured, then kissed her.

It was a brief kiss, but reassuring all the same.

''You're not mad?'' she whispered.

''I got over it. We'll work things out, sweetheart. Okay?''

She nodded, then turned to greet Lady Hereford. Soon all four of them were eating the food Maisie had sent. Liz thought she'd never had so lovely a picnic. Pete seemed in the best mood she'd seen yet, teasing both her and Dansky. Even more noticeable was his attitude toward his mother.

Though she thought he loved his mother, Liz had noticed a tension between the two. Today it was gone. Pete talked with affection about his childhood in England and encouraged his mother to speak of Robert and the Hereford estate.

"Perhaps when we leave Cargenia, you can accompany us to England to visit Hereford, Beth. I'd like you to meet Robert."

"And Celia," Lady Hereford added hurriedly. "Robert's wife. A lovely girl of course. Perhaps by then they will be expecting an heir."

"Not bloody likely," Pete muttered, sounding more British than cowboy for the first time.

"You don't like Celia?" Liz asked.

"No."

"Now, Peter, you are too hard on the girl. After all, she and Robert have been married less than a year. She'll adjust."

"Oh, she's not used to having a title?" Liz asked, feeling sympathy for a fellow sufferer.

"That's not the problem," Pete said. "She's not used to being human."

"Peter!" his mother protested.

The day before Pete would've walked away in anger at his mother's rebuke. Today he smiled in apology. "Forgive me, Mother. Maybe I'm wrong. I hope so. I want Robert to be happy."

"So do I, Peter, dear."

The two smiled at each other and Liz knew something had occurred to change things between them.

Looking around for a different subject, she stared at the lake. "Do you fish here?"

"Yeah, when I have time. Sometimes I camp here overnight and fish at sunrise. It's terrific. After we're married, maybe we'll do that."

Liz caught her breath. He'd spoken as if their marriage was a sure thing. She looked quickly at his mother, as well as Pete. Neither seemed aware of the importance of his words. Dansky, however, was staring at Pete, a speculative look on his face.

She gulped a breath of air. "That...that would be nice."

"Do you fish, or is that something else Dansky forbids?" Pete asked.

Fortunately for Liz, Dansky picked up his cue. "Her Highness has fished on occasion in Scotland."

"Really? I'm impressed," Pete said with a grin. "I thought you wouldn't want to get dirty."

Liz stuck out her tongue at him and Dansky frowned.

"Her Highness was helping to promote tourism," he said, looking sternly at Liz.

She shrugged in response to his silent reprimand. So a princess wouldn't stick out her tongue. Too bad for the princess. "I would like to camp. Do you have a tent?"

"Sure. A small one. You wouldn't mind sharing, would you?"

Pete's gaze contained all kinds of messages, most of them X-rated. Her cheeks burned as she replied. "No, I wouldn't mind."

"Of course, there would only be room for two people," he added, winking at her.

"Behave yourself, Peter. You're embarrassing Beth. He's a naughty boy, my dear, but a precious one."

"Now you're embarrassing *me,* Mother," Pete complained good-naturedly.

Dansky didn't seem amused by their give-and-take. He concentrated on his food, not speaking.

"Are you enjoying the sandwiches, Dansky?" Liz asked.

"Yes, they are quite tasty, Your Highness."

"Wait until you taste the dessert. Maisie made oatmeal raisin cookies, my favorite," Pete added.

"Perhaps we could take a stroll around the lake before we eat—"

Liz's suggestion was cut off by a blinding flash of lightning followed almost at once by a loud thunderous roll.

Chapter Thirteen

Pete's head snapped up and he studied the sky. "Damn! I didn't check the weather forecast today with all the craziness we've had. Let's pack up."

"Don't we have a little time before the storm arrives?" Liz asked, wondering about the sternness of his order.

"No. The storm looks as if it's moving fast and packing a wallop. I don't think we'll make it back to the house before it hits." While he spoke, he threw the residue of their lunch back into the saddlebags. "Dansky, get the ladies mounted, please."

In two minutes they were all on horseback and rapidly leaving the lake behind. Pete urged them up the trail at a hard lope, bringing up the rear.

They were halfway home when the rain began. It fell in sheets, making it difficult to see where they were going. They were descending the second hill, and the trail became treacherous, their mounts slipping and sliding several times.

Pete caught up to Liz and shouted, "We have to keep going until we're on flat land, at least."

She nodded, not bothering to answer. Her hat shielded her eyes somewhat, but she was drenched and quickly growing chilled. Even in summer Montana could be cool. And with the rain, they were all losing body heat.

When they finally reached pastureland, Pete rode ahead to talk to his mother. Then he dropped back to Liz's side. "We've decided to go on. There's no shelter here and we're all wet, anyway."

Again Liz nodded. She couldn't see the ranch house through the rain, and she tried to remember how far it was. Their mounts were winded from their run and it became necessary to walk them. She hung on to the saddle horn, feeling her strength drain from her.

At some point Pete reached for her reins and began leading her mount, shouting encouraging words. She tried to smile, to let him know she would hang in there, but she had to duck her head against the driving rain.

Without Pete's presence Liz knew she would've been frightened by the sudden deluge. It was easy to become disoriented in a storm. But as long as Pete was beside her, she felt safe.

When she'd exhausted her reserve of strength, buffeted by the storm almost to the point of unconsciousness, Pete pulled her horse to a halt. She struggled to lift her head and was relieved to see they'd reached the back porch of the ranch house.

As she began to dismount, she found Pete beside her, reaching up to lift her down and guide her to the shelter of the back porch.

Maisie held the door open and wrapped warm towels around everyone's shoulders as they entered. Liz couldn't remember feeling anything as good as that towel. Wiping her face with the ends even as she kept the towel around her shoulders, she turned to thank Pete for his help and discovered he hadn't come in with them.

"Where's Pete?"

"He's taking the horses to the barn," Maisie explained.

"But he's drenched, like the rest of us!"

"Bless you, honey, he's used to that," the housekeeper said.

"Maisie's right, Beth," Lady Hereford assured her. "Pete will be all right."

Although she knew the two older women were probably right about Pete's ability to withstand the rigors of a rainstorm, Liz would feel better when he came back to the house. "Will he be there long?"

"In the barn? Probably. He'll want to wipe down the tack after he cares for the horses. And there may be other problems to deal with, thanks to the storm," Maisie added, staring out the window.

"Was it expected?" Lady Hereford asked.

"Not really, until about an hour ago. I had the radio on and the weatherman started talking about a possibly violent storm moving into the area."

Liz still stared out the window while Dansky and Lady Hereford sipped the hot coffee Maisie had made.

"Why don't you three go have a hot shower and

change into dry clothes? Pete will be along when he can.'' Maisie began mopping up the floor by the door.

Liz reluctantly followed the other two up the stairs. A hot shower would feel good, but she wished she'd gone to the barn with Pete. With less than forty-eight hours now before her adventure ended, she wanted to spend every minute with Pete she could. Even if that wasn't the wisest choice she could make.

PETE DIDN'T GET BACK to the house until long after dark. He'd had to make sure all his men returned safely and then get an update as to conditions for his animals. The storm had rotten timing. Not only had it ruined their picnic, but tomorrow, Beth's last full day on the ranch, he'd have to be out in the saddle checking for damage.

He stepped into the warmth of the kitchen and discovered Beth waiting for him. With an anxious cry she hurried to his side. He couldn't imagine a sweeter greeting even though he held her away from him. ''Watch out. You'll get wet all over again.''

Beth snatched a towel off a nearby chair and wiped his face before wrapping the towel around him. ''Are you all right?''

''Sure. Were you worried about me?''

She lay her head against his soaked chest, holding on to his shoulders. ''Yes,'' she whispered.

He stroked her head and kissed her forehead. ''Thanks, sweetheart, but you shouldn't have been. A little rain's not going to do me in.''

''That's what Maisie said,'' Beth told him, raising

her head and smiling, "but I was about ready to start building an ark. And it's still raining."

"Yeah. We heard the weather report on the radio in the barn. Looks like it's going to continue for several more hours."

"You must be starved," Beth said. "We saved you some of Maisie's roast beef. Do you want a hot shower first?"

"I reckon I'd better. I don't think I smell too good." He grinned at Beth as he released her and headed for the stairs. "But it won't take long. Five minutes."

True to his word, he was soon back downstairs ready to devour anything set on the table. To his surprise he discovered two places set. "Who else hasn't eaten? It's after ten already."

"I waited to eat with you," Beth replied as she put a bowl of mashed potatoes on the table.

"Sweetheart, you shouldn't have waited. But I'm glad you did," he added, smiling warmly at her, thinking about the strange combination she represented. He'd never have imagined Princess Elsbeth sacrificing any comfort for him. Yet, as Beth, he'd found his princess to be a warm, thoughtful woman.

"It didn't seem fair to be comfortable and warm and eat, too, when you were suffering."

"I didn't suffer all that much. We all shared Maisie's cookies," he informed her with a grin.

One slim eyebrow shot up. "Oh, no! I'd hoped to have those cookies for dessert."

He immediately felt badly until he noticed Beth's

grin. "I was about to apologize, but you're smiling. What am I missing here?"

"Maisie had lots more cookies for us," Beth confessed. Then she slipped an arm around his waist and pulled him to the table. "Come on and eat while the roast beef is hot."

A few minutes later Pete shoved his chair back from the table with a satisfied sigh.

"Full?" Beth asked.

Without even thinking about his actions, he leaned over and kissed her, enjoying the taste of her more than the roast beef, although it had certainly been good. "Mmm-hmm. That was delicious, and the company was good, too, Beth. Thanks for waiting for me."

"I'm glad I did. I could enjoy it more knowing you weren't still working."

He wrapped an arm around her shoulders. To his surprise she laid her head on his shoulder as if it was a common occurrence. The rightness of it all reinforced his decision that whatever the cost, marriage to Beth was his only choice.

Pushing back her soft wavy hair, he kissed her neck and whispered, "What shall we do now? Want to try out my mattress?"

"Pete!" she protested, but he thought he could hear in her voice a wanting that matched his own.

He straightened in his chair. "Where are your shadows?"

She understood his meaning at once. "They've already retired for the night. The ride wore Dansky out. Petrocelli—"

"Dansky is more tired than you? Why haven't *you* given out, sweetheart? You're less used to riding than he is."

Her cheeks reddened and he wondered at the cause.

"I had a nap earlier."

"Ah." That explained it. She'd probably slept all afternoon. "Did we have a lot more calls from that article in the paper?"

"It hasn't been too bad."

"Good. As long as we refuse to talk to anyone, curiosity should die down." As if to contradict him, the phone rang.

"Damn it, don't they ever give up?" He moved to the phone, waving Beth back into her chair. "Palisades Ranch."

"You don't sound too happy, little brother."

"Robert! Is everything all right?" Pete and his brother didn't talk often, but he missed him.

"I'm not doing as well as you, if the picture I saw is any indication."

His words were spoken with humor, but Pete heard an undercurrent of concern. "You worried?"

"I tried to talk to Mother before she left. I don't want you pushed into anything."

"Don't worry. I'm not going to let her do the same thing to me. Beth is different." They were speaking shorthand, but they understood each other perfectly.

"Things could be worse. I have big news. Celia is expecting."

Pete's heart filled at the thought of Robert being a father, even if he had to share the event with the wretched Celia. "Congratulations, old man. When?"

"Another seven months. I'm not going to tell Mother until she returns."

"Does this make things better between you and Celia?"

There was a long silence, and Pete had his answer before Robert said lightly, "Pregnant ladies are cranky."

Pete had already experienced Celia cranky. He couldn't imagine her being worse. "Bad luck, brother."

"Just be sure you're making the right decision," Robert said earnestly. "I want you to be happy."

Pete looked over his shoulder at Beth, his gaze warming. She was nothing like his brother's wife. Nothing at all. "I am. I'm hoping Beth can come visit after I go to Cargenia this summer. You'll like her."

"I'll look forward to meeting her. Take care and give Mother my love."

Pete hung up the phone, then reached for Beth and pulled her into his arms.

"Is everything all right?"

"My brother is going to be a father, but we've got to keep that quiet. He's not going to tell Mother until she returns to England."

"She and Maisie will be thrilled."

"Yeah. Have you thought about having kids?" He rested his chin on her silky hair, waiting for her answer.

"Yes. And more than one. I was an only child."

"I know that," he said with a chuckle, but wondered about the sudden movement she made, as if she'd forgotten something. "You okay?"

"Yes, of course. Just tired. I think I'll go up to bed."

She tried to withdraw from his arms, but he kept her at his side. "I'll join you. In fact, I'll really join you if you want, and we can start making those babies tonight."

Her cheeks flamed and she again tried to pull away.

"No, thank you," she said sedately, as if she were refusing a cup of tea.

"You don't know what you're missing," he teased, wishing he had no conscience and could sweep her into his arms and overrule her polite words.

Her gaze tested his resolve as she smiled and said, "I know."

How tempting it was for Liz to agree to his suggestion, to tell him she only wanted him, forever and ever. To tell him she loved him and always would. All true. But not as the princess. The princess who would secure his future for him, who would provide him with the deed to his beloved ranch.

If she took her pleasure, she would betray the man she loved. If she didn't go to his bed, she would disappoint him now, but maybe he wouldn't hate her when he learned the truth.

Regretfully she backed out of his embrace. "No, I don't think our going to your bed would be a good idea."

"Are you sure? Because I think it would be a great idea," he assured her with a chuckle.

Hoping for a lighter ending to their evening, she punched him in the chest. "You'd probably fall asleep, anyway."

His face grew serious. "Not before we become one in every sense of the word, for all time, sweetheart." Then he grinned. "Afterward, I wouldn't make any promises."

"We'll wait," Liz promised, knowing she was lying, but having no choice. "When the time is right, we'll make love, and it will be the most beautiful moment of my life."

He kissed her, a kiss of sweetness, of promise. "Guaranteed, my love, guaranteed."

THE PHONE STARTED RINGING half an hour before his alarm sounded the next morning. Pete finally abandoned the bed for the shower, where he couldn't hear the ringing.

After he was back in his bedroom pulling on a fresh pair of jeans, the phone rang again. Irritated, he snatched up the receiver. "Hello?"

"I want to speak to Dansky."

Something about the woman's voice sounded familiar, but he wasn't in the mood to be friendly. "Dansky's in bed. Call back at a decent hour."

"I will speak to Dansky now!" the imperious voice ordered.

"No, you will not." Without waiting for a response, he placed the receiver back on the cradle. A niggle of concern filled him as he realized he hadn't even asked if the call was an emergency. But the voice hadn't sounded disturbed. Only annoyed and demanding. Poor Dansky. Maybe *all* his calls were like that.

With a shrug Pete picked up a shirt and pulled it

over his head, tucking it into his jeans as he moved toward the door. The phone stopped him.

"Damn it. Don't these people ever sleep?" He picked up the receiver. "What?"

"Do not hang up the phone," the same female voice ordered. "I must speak to Dansky!"

"Look, lady, it's only six o'clock here. Dansky had a rough day yesterday. Give me your name and I'll have him call you when he gets up."

"You think it is more important that he sleep rather than talk to me?" she asked.

"Are you his wife—or his mother?"

She gasped. "No, I am not. Now bring him to the phone!"

"Who's calling?"

"I do not care to reveal that information."

"And I do not care to wake Dansky without it."

"Tell him...tell him his friend from Los Angeles is calling."

"Fine. I'll tell him and he can call you when he's awake." He hung up.

He was doing Dansky a favor, giving him some breathing space from the woman. If the man was thinking of marrying her, he'd better think again.

The phone rang once more.

He couldn't believe the woman's persistence.

"Yes?"

"If you dare to hang up on me again, I shall report you to the owner and you will be out of a job."

"Really? Is that how you deal with anyone who displeases you? Threaten to get them fired?"

"Yes. Call Dansky to the phone at once."

Even if the woman told him it was an emergency now, he wouldn't do as she asked. She'd roused his stubborn streak. "Nope."

"He will be most displeased when he discovers you have not obeyed me."

"It won't be the first time I've displeased him. I'll tell him you called, but that's all I'm going to do, no matter how many times you call. So don't bother me." Again he hung up. Poor Dansky. Too bad he hadn't found someone as sweet and considerate as Beth. Even if the man occasionally irritated Pete, he didn't think anyone should have to put up with a woman like this caller.

In fact, Pete believed everyone should have a princess for his wife. Just as he intended to do.

Chapter Fourteen

The rain had stopped when Liz crawled from her comfortable nest of bedcovers. Checking her watch, she realized she'd slept later than she'd intended. The idea of having breakfast with Pete before he started his workday had filled her mind as she'd gone to sleep.

But Pete had already been at work for a couple of hours. She dressed and hurried downstairs, hoping she wouldn't make too much extra work for Maisie.

Though she was the last to come downstairs, Liz discovered both her escorts and Lady Hereford just beginning breakfast. "Good morning. I'm sorry I'm so late, Maisie."

"No problem, Beth. I'm making pancakes. Yours'll be ready in a coupla minutes."

Liz poured her own coffee and juice and joined the others at the table. "Is everyone feeling all right after our adventure yesterday?"

"Of course I am," Lady Hereford assured her. "Your friend Dansky thinks he's catching a cold, however. How about you?"

"I feel fine. I'm sorry, Dansky. Are you running a fever?"

"I don't know," the man said gruffly. "I'm not used to such difficult circumstances."

"Then you'd better never plan on workin' as a cowboy," Maisie said, carrying a plate of pancakes to Liz. "Cowboys get rained on a lot."

Dansky gave a grimace but didn't speak. Instead, he took a big bite of Maisie's pancakes.

"Pete worked a lot longer before he got out of his wet clothes. I hope he doesn't catch a cold," Liz reminded her henchman. He was acting as if he'd been mistreated on purpose.

"I'm sure Pete is used to such trials, Your Highness. You must not worry about him. It might spoil your trip home," Petrocelli said.

Liz recognized his reminder that her time here at the ranch, pretending to be the princess, was almost over. She stared at him, raising her chin. "I believe I will always be concerned with Pete's safety...and happiness."

"It is useless to worry when there is nothing you can do," he said.

"Perhaps there is something I can do," Liz returned, determined not to let him have the last word, forgetting how much Pete could lose if he chose not to marry the absent princess.

"Of course there is, dear," Lady Hereford intervened cheerfully. "You can marry him. That will make him happy."

Jerked from her fantasy world, where she rescued Pete from a loveless marriage and warmed his bed for the rest of her days, Liz gulped and attempted a smile. ''Of course.''

Petrocelli, unlike Dansky, who remained occupied with his breakfast, still stared at Liz. In an attempt at a silent apology, she nodded to him and then concentrated on her breakfast. There was nothing else she could do, either to reassure Petrocelli or to rescue Pete.

But she wished there was.

PETE HAD BEEN in the saddle for eight hours already, and it would take another three just to get back to the barn. He reined in Diamond and reached into his saddlebag for one of the sandwiches Maisie had had ready for him when he left the house that morning.

''Time for a break, Harvey. You still got food?''

''Yep. I think I may be gettin' too old for this life, boy. My bones are achin'.'' Even as he complained, Harvey wrapped a leg around the saddle horn with the agility of a young man.

Pete grinned. He'd heard those words before. ''You can go back now if you need to, Harvey.''

''And leave you out here on your own? Get real! You're still wet behind the ears. Someone has to guide you!''

They'd both known Harvey wouldn't desert Pete. He frequently groused about whatever was occupying his time, but he was one of the hardest workers Pete had.

They sat their saddles, chewing the sandwiches, letting their mounts graze. Little conversation was exchanged, as if they were conserving their energy.

They were headed for a particular area that concerned Pete. It was hard to reach, but because of the excellent grass in the area, a large herd grazed there. Pete wanted to be sure none of the cows had gotten into trouble. The creek that bordered one side of the pasture frequently overran its banks.

Shortly they moved on. A half hour later as they approached the creek, the dull roar that filled their ears told its story.

"Uh-oh," Harvey muttered. "Sounds like a powerful train."

"Yeah," Pete agreed. But he said nothing else until they reached its banks. While it had overflowed at some point, indicated by the flat grass and debris, the creek was back in its banks, but it was deep and angry.

"I see some of the herd," Harvey shouted over the noise.

"Yeah, but not many of them. I think Diamond can make it across. I'm going to go check on them. Why don't you wait here?"

"Are you saying Diamond is better than Sweet Potato, here?" Harvey asked, referring to his sorrel gelding.

"Nope. But there's no need for both of us to get wet."

"Lead on, boss, and stop being silly. I want to head back to the barn before it gets too dark to find the way."

Pete did as he was told. He'd been doubtful he could prevent Harvey from crossing the creek, but he'd tried. Guiding Diamond toward the trail that had once led to an easy crossing, he plunged into the fast-moving stream, cold water splashing him as he guided his horse to the far bank.

The powerful tug of the current made it hard for Diamond to keep his footing. Pete held his breath, knowing how dangerous it would be if Diamond went down.

His gaze fixed on the other side and the cattle he could see, Pete forgot his fears as they neared the other bank and so was unprepared for Diamond's stumble. One minute he was in control, the next he'd fallen from the saddle like the greenest dude.

When he hit the water, he discovered what had caused Diamond's misstep. Because of the strength of the water, Diamond had missed the trail up the bank and tried to climb out a few feet past it. Boulders were in the way.

Pete's head slammed into one of them and he saw stars. When he came to, he seemed to be going down for the third time, choking and gasping for air. He waved his arms, trying to find a hold to grab on to, give him time for a much needed breath.

A hand grabbed his shirtfront and his face broke water. With a monumental heave Harvey pulled him to the top of the bank and collapsed beside him on the grass, coughing.

"Harvey?" he called faintly, gasping for breath, surprised at how weak his voice sounded. "You okay?"

"I reckon I should be askin' you that question, boss. I thought you were gonna reach the Gulf of Mexico before I could grab you."

"Yeah, thanks, man. I think you just saved my life."

"Aw, you woulda made it," Harvey assured him with true cowboy modesty.

"Where's Diamond?" Pete demanded, remembering his horse's struggle. "Is he all right?"

"He was climbing out as I grabbed you," Harvey assured him, sitting up to look around. Both horses were standing together a few feet away, looking spent. "There they are."

The two men struggled to their feet, Harvey offering Pete an arm that he ignored, and turned to their mounts.

Diamond shied away as Pete reached for him, an unusual occurrence. Pete knew at once something was wrong. "Easy, boy, easy," he murmured, reaching for the reins. As he did, he saw blood on the grass. Hurriedly he checked his horse and discovered a large gash on Diamond's chest. "Harvey!"

"Yeah, boss?" Harvey asked as he swung into the saddle.

"Look at this."

Harvey dismounted and joined Pete to examine the horse. "Man, that's nasty."

"Yeah. We've got to bind it so it'll stop bleeding." Pete took a soggy handkerchief from his jean pocket and carefully folded it into a pad to cover the cut. "Hold it in place for me."

Harvey did as Pete asked, watching as his boss stripped off his shirt and tried to reach around the horse's chest to tie the makeshift bandage in place.

When the sleeves wouldn't meet, Harvey stripped off his own shirt. "Here, tie them together."

Pete didn't protest. Diamond was too good a horse to worry about sacrificing a shirt. If they didn't get the blood flow stopped and keep the cut clean, the horse might die.

He might die, anyway, Pete realized grimly. There was no way Diamond could make the long trek back to the house in his condition, even if he could cross the stream again. "Harvey, you're going to have to go for help."

"You should come with me. You may have a concussion. Old Sweet Potato can carry double."

"I can't leave Diamond. I want you to get back to the house as quick as you can and find the doc. You'll need to bring him in from the back side in the morning with a trailer."

"And leave you out here all night with no shirt? You'll catch your death!"

"I'll be fine. Leave me some matches and whatever food you've got left." He wasn't looking forward to an uncomfortable night, but it wasn't much of a sacrifice if it saved Diamond's life.

Harvey stared at Diamond, then finally nodded his head. "I'll go, but I'll send someone out here as soon as I can with some provisions and a bedroll."

"You do and I'll fire you. You know everyone'll get back late, after putting in twelve hours in the saddle. I don't want that kind of sacrifice. The night'll be half over, anyway. You just be here as early as you can in the morning with the vet."

With a grimace of acknowledgment, Harvey

slapped Pete on the back. "Okay, boss, but you take care of yourself. I'm afraid your head is messed up."

"A headache is all. Get going now. And be careful on the crossing."

Pete stood beside Diamond and watched Harvey make his way back across, praying that the older cowboy wouldn't run into any problems. Harvey waved after mounting the other bank. Then he headed east toward the ranch.

Pete surveyed his supplies. He had no shirt, a couple of sandwiches, a pack of dry matches and an injured horse. Not exactly what he would've chosen for a camp out. He picked a spot surrounded by boulders near the edge of the creek for his campsite. The boulders would reflect the heat of the fire he intended to build. And they would offer protection from any animals drawn by the scent of blood and seeking an easy kill.

Pete unsaddled Diamond and put the saddle by the rocks. Then he spread the saddle blanket on top of the rocks to dry in what sunlight remained. That would be his only cover for the cold night.

Then he filled his hat with creek water and set it near the rocks. Leading a weakened Diamond over, he tethered the horse beside the rocks near the hat. He needed to keep the animal tied in case predators spooked him.

After making those arrangements, he began gathering firewood. It was all wet, which, if it didn't dry out by sunset, was going to make building a fire tough. He laid as many pieces as he could on the rocks. The rest he stacked on the ground.

All the while, his head throbbed more and more. He knew the movement wasn't going to ease his pain, but he had no choice. Not if he wanted both he and his horse to make it to sunrise. When his preparations were done, he took his rifle and leaned it against the rock, sitting down beside it.

He guessed he only had another hour of sunlight. Time to give his head a rest and hope some of the wood dried out before the sun set.

The plans he'd made for this evening, a dinner out and some time alone with Beth, were gone now. He only hoped he got back in time to tell her goodbye—for a month.

Otherwise, he was going to have to kiss his horse, instead of his girl.

LIZ HATED THE DAY. She took turns with Petrocelli answering the phone. The rest of the time she hid in the house from the reporters who were constantly coming to the door. Each time Dansky routed them, but she was beginning to feel trapped.

Lady Hereford still contended that the publicity would be good, but she couldn't convince anyone to agree. She offered to answer the phone, but Liz was afraid she would say something inappropriate, so she refused the offer.

However, when Petrocelli had taken a break, going upstairs, a call from the King of Cargenia, her supposed father, had her racing to the front door for Dansky.

"It's the king," she hissed as he closed the door from another importunate reporter.

"Where's Petrocelli?" Dansky asked urgently as he hurried down the hall.

"Upstairs."

"Get him. There was another car coming up the drive. He'll have to get rid of them."

Liz knew she certainly couldn't answer the door. After that picture of the princess had appeared in the tabloid, all the reporters would recognize her at once.

She rushed up the stairs just as the doorbell rang. "Petrocelli!" she called softly, tapping on his door.

It swung open. For the first time, she saw Petrocelli with his tie loosened and his coat off. "Yes?"

"Dansky had to answer the phone because the king called, and there are more reporters arriving. They've already rung the doorbell."

He rushed across the room to grab his coat and follow her down the hall. They reached the downstairs hall in time to wave Maisie back to the kitchen. Petrocelli swung open the door to address the waiting group of reporters as Liz hid.

"Gentlemen, we would appreciate your leaving the property immediately. Lord Peter has left orders to call the authorities if you trespass."

Though the reporters were clearly not happy with Petrocelli's request, as evidenced by their grumbling, they headed for their vehicle.

As he closed the door, Liz asked, "Shouldn't we see if Dansky is still on the phone?"

Petrocelli nodded and hurried down the hall to Pete's office, Liz right behind him.

Dansky was just replacing the receiver as they entered.

"What did he want?" Liz asked.

"He has seen the photo."

"Already? How? Did he realize—" She broke off when Dansky shook his head. She'd been sure it would take at least a week for the picture to be reprinted in Europe.

"The photographer offered it simultaneously here in the States and in Cargenia."

"Was he angry?" Liz asked, wondering if his reaction would be like Lady Hereford's.

"Not at all. In fact, he thought more pictures would be a good thing," Dansky said, frowning. He turned to Petrocelli. "I tried to change his mind. Even after I told him the marriage was facing some difficulties, he thought the publicity, even if the marriage didn't come off, would do Cargenia some good."

"But we can't allow the pictures!" Petrocelli exclaimed. "Miss Caine is remarkably like the princess, but I think her father would see the differences, even if others did not."

"True. I told the king that Her Highness had caught a cold from our ride yesterday and was not particularly photogenic at the moment." He turned to Liz. "Should he call again, please remember to sneeze a couple of times."

"Surely he won't call before I leave tomorrow. What time shall we go?" Liz experienced pain at even thinking of leaving Pete, but she had no choice.

"I arranged for the limo to return at ten in the morning. That will give us plenty of time to catch our plane at noon. Your flight leaves only fifteen minutes earlier."

She nodded and turned toward the door.

"Where are you going?" Petrocelli asked.

"I need to get out of the house. I'm beginning to feel the walls close in on me." Without waiting for their approval she left the office.

When she reached the kitchen, Maisie and Lady Hereford were sitting at the table enjoying a cup of coffee and a chat.

"Want some coffee?" Maisie offered.

"Would you object if I took a cup with me?"

"With you?" Lady Hereford asked. "Where are you going?"

"While we're between callers, I thought I'd walk down to the barn. It's almost five. Surely Pete will be coming in fairly soon."

"Doubt it," Maisie said, shaking her head. "He probably won't be in until about dark, if then. There's a lot of land to cover, and he's not one to neglect his herd." She paused and then added, "I know he'll want to spend time with you, but he might even spend the night out on the land, if he's too far away."

"You mean he might not come back until tomorrow? But we have to leave at ten!" She hadn't intended to sound so forlorn, but Liz couldn't bear the thought of not seeing him again.

Lady Hereford seemed much less affected. "Don't worry, child. He can call you after you get home, and we'll be arriving next month. You'll have a lot of time together then."

Liz bit her bottom lip, hoping to hold back the protest that rose in her. No, *she* wouldn't talk to Pete or spend a lot of time with him. All she had was today and tomorrow morning. And Pete was somewhere in the pastures spending his time with cows.

"I...I think I'll go down to the barn, anyway. It would be nice to get away from the phone calls and the reporters."

"Just you be careful, Beth," Maisie warned. "Sometimes they nose around where they shouldn't."

Liz smiled grimly and poured herself a cup of coffee. "I'll be careful. And I'll bring back your mug safe and sound." Then she left the house.

She managed to cover the distance between the house and barn before any more reporters showed up. Slipping into the dim light of the barn, she was reminded of her first visit to it, carried by Pete. He'd kissed her there.

If she'd known then the pain she would suffer at Pete's hands, however unintentional, would she have stayed? She ruefully acknowledged that she would have. She'd accepted a fee and promised to do a job.

And besides, even if she never saw Pete again, she'd always love him. She'd always know that true love existed. She'd always remember his touch.

To think of missing such delights, of never having met Pete, was more than she could bear to contemplate.

There weren't many occupants of the barn today. Because it was summer, only several mares due to foal were being kept in. Liz petted the animals and wandered around the barn, enjoying the scents and sights she connected to her father. Many a time she'd gone with him to deal with sick animals, even acting as his assistant as she'd grown older.

At one point she'd considered becoming a vet, too. But then she'd caught the acting bug and headed for Hollywood. Her father had never made her feel she'd let him down, though. Both parents had encouraged her to pursue her dream.

Which had led her to heartbreak.

She shrugged and settled down on a bale of hay that provided her with a view toward the west, the direction from which Pete would arrive. Sipping her coffee, she dreamed of the hours spent with Pete, hardly aware of the passing time.

Just as she realized dusk was approaching, she caught sight of a single rider racing across the pasture. Remembering Pete talk about keeping the riders in pairs in case something went wrong, Liz knew at once there was a problem.

She set down her mug and hurried outside to open the nearby gate to the corral. As the rider approached, she identified him as Harvey. Harvey without his shirt.

Where was Pete? And what had gone wrong?

Chapter Fifteen

The first question Liz asked was the one closest to her heart. "Where's Pete?"

She didn't even know if Harvey had been riding with Pete, but she wanted to be sure of his safety.

"Across Harmony Creek," Harvey answered as he swung off his mount. "His horse is injured. I gotta call the vet."

"What do you mean injured? Is Pete okay?"

"Maybe a concussion. Diamond has a gash in his chest. He's lost some blood." All the time Harvey was talking he was hurrying to the barn.

Liz went after him, standing beside him as he called the vet. The man was out on a case and his wife wasn't sure when he'd get back. Harvey left a message, telling the woman he'd pick the vet up at four in the morning.

When he hung up the phone, Liz got right to the most important point. "You're leaving Pete out there alone?"

"Don't have a choice. We'll have to come in on the back side of the ranch to get to him. We'll be driving at least three hours, pulling a trailer, after I pick up the vet. I couldn't ride all night out to Pete and back and still make that trip. Besides, he said he'd fire me if I sent any of the boys out to him.''

"Why?"

"Because they'll all be exhausted and they couldn't get there until midnight, anyway. None of them have come in, have they?"

"No."

"Well, they probably won't until eight or nine."

"Then I'll go." She began to head toward the house, eager to ready herself for the ride.

"Hold on, Princess. Pete'd kill me if I let you go."

She spun around, using her royal air. "Dear Harvey, you can't stop me. It will make it easier for me if you give me directions, but I'll find him or die trying, whether you tell me or not."

He scratched the back of his head. "I reckon I'd best give you directions, then, 'cause Pete sure don't want you to die. But it's gonna be cold. And there might be predators comin' around. Can you fire a gun?"

"Yes. Find what I'll need while I change clothes and get some food from Maisie."

"You might get some more clothes for Pete. He got dunked in the creek and used our shirts to wrap up Diamond."

"He's out there shirtless and wet, with night coming on?" Liz asked, horrified.

"Yes'm. So find him a change of clothes, too."

On the way to the house, Liz considered her options. If she revealed her plan to her escorts, they would forbid it. Even Lady Hereford might recommend she stay at the house. But she could trust Maisie to understand.

When she entered the kitchen and found the cook alone, she said, "Maisie, I'll need food, hot coffee in a thermos and probably some aspirin, packed for a horseback ride."

"What's wrong?" Maisie asked.

"Pete's horse has a gash in its chest. He's staying out all night with the animal until the vet can get there, and he may have a concussion. I'm going out to him." She paused and stared at Maisie. "I'll need you to cover for me. Tell everyone I've gone to bed with a sick headache or something."

"Are you sure you should go? One of the boys…"

"They won't be back for at least two or three hours. I can reach Pete by then. Harvey is going to hook up a trailer and pick up the vet at four in the morning so they can reach Pete as soon as it's daylight. I'm the only one who can go."

And she wanted to do this for Pete. God had given her a chance to see Pete again and she wasn't about to be deprived of it.

She hurried upstairs to change into jeans and boots. She added a warm sweater to pull over her shirt when the sun went down. Then she crossed the hall to Pete's room. Pulling open drawers until she found all she needed, she carried the bundle downstairs.

In the meantime Maisie had brought out a sleeping bag. She took the clothing away from Liz and rolled them up in the sleeping bag. In a saddlebag she'd packed a thermos of coffee and food. Then she handed Liz a canteen filled with water.

"What about something for protection?"

"Harvey's going to find me a rifle to take. He's waiting for me at the barn."

Maisie hugged her, to Liz's surprise. "You take care of yourself and him, too," she ordered.

Liz smiled. "I will."

She escaped from the kitchen, afraid she'd be seen and prevented from going.

At the barn Harvey had put on a shirt, found a rifle for Liz and added a small bag of medicine and a horse blanket. "Maybe Pete can give Diamond an antibiotic shot."

"We'll manage," she assured him. After listening to his directions, she tied the bedroll on Beauty's back, swung into the saddle before Harvey could help her and headed toward the west and Pete.

CHILLS WOKE PETE. He'd fallen asleep leaning against the boulders. Probably that hadn't been a smart idea, since he might have a concussion. Gingerly feeling his head, he discovered a lump on his forehead that probably made him look like Quasimodo. Fortunately it didn't bother Diamond.

The horse was standing where he'd tied him, his head down. Pete struggled to his feet and stroked the injured animal, offering encouraging words. Then he gathered the wood he'd spread out on the rocks into a pile. With a handful of grass he'd earlier pulled out to dry, he managed to get a fire started.

Even though the fire wasn't very big at first, Pete

welcomed the light and little heat it produced. He sat down with his back to the rocks and draped the horse blanket over his chest. He was worried about Diamond, wishing he had a large blanket with which to cover him, too.

At least Diamond had his coat to keep him warm. The hair on Pete's chest was hardly adequate. He thought about the comfort of his bed at home, yearning for its warmth. While he was about it, he also thought about Beth in his bed.

Though he hadn't experienced that particular comfort, he knew it would be heavenly. His musings were halted by a sound nearby and Diamond's restlessness. A predator was approaching.

Pete eased his hand over to his rifle and stood up, stepping closer to Diamond. He wasn't going to let anything hurt his horse. When he spotted a pair of golden eyes in the dark, he took aim and fired.

Diamond pulled at his tether, but the sound of flight was comforting to Pete. At least for a while they should be left alone.

He laid more pieces of wood on the fire that was still struggling to catch hold. Smoke rose from the logs that weren't quite dry.

"We're both going to need a bath when we get home, boy," he told Diamond. "Beth won't want me near her until I clean up, and probably the mares will feel the same way about you." He stroked Diamond's neck, remembering the hours he'd spent with his horse.

Wishing he had a hot cup of coffee, Pete pulled Diamond a little closer to the fire. Then he reached for the saddle blanket, ready to settle in for the night. He'd checked his watch and saw it was only a little before ten. He didn't figure Harvey and the vet would get there much before eight in the morning, so he had a long night ahead of him.

Just as he was lowering himself to the ground, his knees stiff from their earlier cold bath, he heard another noise. Cursing under his breath, as much from his throbbing head as from the intrusion, he straightened back up, bringing the rifle with him.

Then he frowned. The sound wasn't that of something stirring in the brush. It was coming from a distance away but drawing nearer. If he didn't know better, he'd think it was a horse racing toward them.

Damn it, if Harvey had disobeyed him, he'd...be grateful, he realized. He wasn't feeling too well. A few creature comforts would be welcome, but it was hard to believe anyone could've gotten here this fast after putting in a long day.

Straining his eyes, he almost shouted with relief when he made out the form of a horse and rider moving toward him. Fortunately the creek had gone down considerably since he'd tried to cross that afternoon.

One of his men would have no trouble negotiating the stream. And hopefully keeping sleeping bags dry.

''Hello?'' he called out.

''Pete?'' the rider called in return.

He froze, stunned by the identity of the rider. That wasn't the manly tone of one of his cowboys. It was the sexy voice that filled his dreams. Beth's.

He charged toward the creek. ''Beth? What the hell are you doing here? Don't you even think of crossing the creek!'' It had gone down, but it might still be risky for a novice rider like Beth.

And he wasn't in any condition to play hero.

She ignored him and started down the far bank.

''Beth!'' he shouted again, though his head felt as if it was almost splitting open. ''Beth, go back!''

His only answer was a splash as Beauty hit the water. Unable to speak again, he held his breath as the horse steadily crossed the stream, then climbed the embankment.

Grabbing the reins to pull Beauty forward, Pete's heart was pounding as if he'd just run a marathon. Before he could move Beth slipped from the saddle and threw her arms around him.

''Are you all right?'' she asked. ''I've brought supplies. And something for you to put on. Come on. Let's go over by the fire and unpack.''

When he could finally speak he cried, ''Are you crazy? You had no business risking that crossing! You could've drowned. I told Harvey not to—''

She covered his mouth with her hand. ''Shh. I bet you're making your headache worse.''

He couldn't argue with that. He moved as she urged him toward the fire, but his anger hadn't gone away. Or his fright.

''How dare Harvey let you come here on your own. You could've gotten lost. Or some wild animal could've hurt you. Or you might've fallen off.''

''Or some aliens might've sucked me up into their space craft and impregnated me.''

He ignored her ridiculous statement. ''Harvey is going to—''

"Harvey didn't do anything wrong. He told me not to come. I told him I was coming, anyway. He could give me directions or leave me to wander around out here all night looking for you. He was kind enough to give me directions. Now stop fussing and put on these clothes." She'd been unrolling a sleeping bag while she talked.

Pete automatically took whatever she thrust at him. When he discovered a shirt, jacket, underwear, socks and jeans, he managed a thank-you. After all, his jeans were still wet, as were his socks.

"Do you want coffee before you change?" Beth asked casually, as if she wasn't offering a miracle.

"Yes! Please."

"Good. You can use the coffee to swallow some pain pills for your head."

"How did you know my head hurts?"

"Harvey said you might have a concussion. I also brought food," she added. "As soon as you take these pills and get a little coffee down you, you can have a roast-beef sandwich."

His mouth watered. "I should've said thank-you at once, Beth, honey, but I was scared you'd put yourself in danger coming out here, and…and it made me angry." He really was feeling like an ungrateful wretch now. She was offering him so much!

She seemed to understand how he felt. She handed him the coffee and two pills. "Don't worry about it. I won't take the coffee back if you're not nice. Take care of yourself and I'll see about Diamond."

He frowned as he thought about her words. What would she know about taking care of an injured animal? He turned around, feeling as if he was moving in slow motion, and he thought Beth was giving Diamond a shot. He shook his head to clear it, but that only increased the ache.

"What are you doing?"

"Harvey said Diamond needed an antibiotic shot."

"But you don't know how to give it," he stated firmly. He knew that much. She was a princess.

"Harvey told me how."

And it was that simple? Before he could puzzle out what was happening, he watched Beth spread a large horse blanket over Diamond, one that covered everything but the horse's head and neck. "You knew to bring a blanket for him?"

"Harvey packed it. He thought of everything."

"Except a way to keep you safe at home."

"I'm a big girl, Pete. I can take care of myself."

Something wasn't right. But his head was hurting so badly he couldn't think. Maybe he was dreaming everything. Maybe the coffee wasn't really here in his hand. Maybe Beth was a figment of his imagination— or his concussion.

"Aren't you changed yet?" she asked, turning back to him.

"No. I… The coffee." He held up the cup as his excuse before taking another sip.

"Maybe you should just strip and get in the sleeping bag. You can put on the clothes in the morning," she said briskly, and began spreading out the sleeping bag, kicking away a rock or two so he'd have a flat surface.

He watched her with fascination, unable to move. Strip? Did she mean he should remove all his clothes?

"Pete," she complained, "you're not moving. Here, sit down and I'll pull off your boots for you." She took his coffee and set it aside before pulling him down to the sleeping bag and tugging on his boots. As soon as she had them off, she removed his socks, too.

"These are still wet. Put on the clean socks. I'll lay these over here."

Pete tugged on the socks, his gaze never leaving Beth. She was much bossier tonight than he'd ever seen her, even at her most royal. But it was a different kind of bossiness. More motherly. But his reaction wasn't of the family sort. When she turned back to him, she reached for the snap on his jeans, which escalated his fantasies.

"Whoa! What—"

"Pete, you need to get out of these wet clothes and into the sleeping bag."

"Where are you going to sleep?" he managed to ask.

For the first time she hesitated. Finally she said, "I only brought one sleeping bag."

"Then we'll share," he asserted, warmth that had nothing to do with dry socks filling him.

"I suppose that makes sense," she said slowly.

"Oh, yeah," Pete agreed. Either the medicine he'd taken was easing his headache, or sexual excitement was a great antidote.

She slid down the zipper of his jeans and began

tugging on his pant legs. "Lift up so your jeans will slide down."

He lay back and lifted his hips from the ground. His arousal was obvious once the denim was removed, and he watched Beth's face as her gaze skimmed his body. Her cheeks flooded with color.

"You know I want you, sweetheart," he said quietly. "I can't hide it."

"I'm trying to take care of you, Pete, so you won't get sick." She turned her back to him and tossed the clean pair of underwear over her shoulder. "Change your underwear and get in the bag. Then I'll bring you your sandwich."

LIZ HOPED PETE didn't see her shaking fingers or he'd know how much she wanted to crawl into the sleeping bag with him. Suddenly she froze. That was exactly what she was going to do. She'd just agreed they would share the sleeping bag to survive the night.

Somehow, surviving and sleeping with Pete hadn't connected until now. She didn't know how she would manage to play the role of nurse when lover was so much more enticing.

Calling to mind all the reasons she'd refused Pete before, she hastened to get out the food she'd promised him. With any luck, after he was fed and warm, Pete would fall asleep and she would be the only one to suffer from their night together.

"Beth?" a deep, sexy voice called. "I'm in the sleeping bag."

She turned around and handed him a wrapped sandwich. "Maisie also sent some oatmeal-raisin cookies."

"Aren't you going to eat?"

"I'll have a cookie or two. I ate in the saddle while we were looking for you."

"We?"

"Beauty and me. I think she wanted to find Diamond as much as I wanted to find you."

"Come over here and sit with me," he invited as he unwrapped his sandwich.

"Shall I get you more coffee first?" she asked.

"Yeah."

He'd pulled his saddle to the head of the sleeping bag as a pillow and sat half-leaning across it, watching her. She poured herself a cup of coffee, as well as refilling his. Then she settled on the end of the sleeping bag, as faraway from him as she could get. "Here are the cookies," she said, dragging a small package from the saddlebag.

"Aren't you cold?" he asked, still watching her.

Liz shot him a look and then studied the fire.

"Oh, no, I'm quite comfortable. You built a good fire. With the rocks behind us I'm very warm."

She sat still as he chewed, refusing to look at him as he ate. The less she looked at him, the stronger her resolve.

"I'd planned on spending the evening with you," he said quietly a few minutes later, "but not like this."

She cast him a nervous smile before turning back to the fire. "Ah, well, the best-laid plans..."

"Yeah. But at least we're together. Without your shadows. How did you get away without them?"

Liz focused her gaze on the fire. "I didn't tell them."

"I guess they'll be upset when they find out."

"Probably."

"I think I'll pass on the cookies, Beth. I'm getting tired."

"Good," she said with relief. His sleeping would relieve some of her pressure. "You can have them for breakfast."

"Okay." He slid down farther into the sleeping bag. "You'd better get ready for bed."

His words sounded so intimate. The thought of slipping into the narrow sleeping bag, her body pressed against his, excited her more than she'd thought possible.

"It'll take a few minutes to get ready." She excused herself and stepped away from the firelight to take care of business. Then she crept quietly back to the campfire, hoping he'd gone to sleep.

Uncertainty filling her, she reached for her jeans fastener. Quickly she stripped off the jeans, then followed with her shirt, before sliding in beside Pete.

Immediately she knew she'd made a mistake.

A mistake she should've recognized before she committed it. What was wrong with her? But she knew the answer. She'd wanted to be one with Pete two days ago. The desire had only gotten stronger. Strong enough to dismiss common sense.

His arm slid under her shoulders and pulled her to him, body to body. Heat suffused her as evidence of his arousal pressed against her and his mouth seized hers.

He wasted no time removing her bra and panties, kicking them to the bottom of the bag and then doing the same to his own underwear. By the time he lifted his lips from hers, Liz was so far lost in a sexual haze she couldn't think of a single reason they shouldn't make love.

Nor, it seemed, could Pete. His mouth sought the tips of her breasts so quickly she couldn't hold back a moan. Pete returned to her lips, whispering words of love before he again kissed her.

As his hands roamed her body, hers returned the favor, delighting in the feel of him, the powerful muscles and raspy hair-covered chest. The frenzy building in her made leisurely enjoyment impossible.

Pete apparently felt the same way because he wasted no time pulling her under him. Only as he sought to make them one, nudging her to open for him, did Liz remember the secret she'd hidden. But it was too late to turn away. Even if her head had been in charge, and it wasn't, she couldn't have denied him.

His lips returned to hers as he plunged into her. The pain was there, briefer than she'd feared, but she couldn't stifle a small cry. He froze, his lips leaving hers as he stared at her in shock.

''Pete...'' she began, unsure how to explain her virginal state.

Before she could continue, his lips covered hers again and his body began to move. Liz was swept away by his touch and a growing friction in her body she'd never experienced before. She was consumed by him, felt as if she were a part of him. When the tension had grown until she thought she couldn't bear it, a crescendo of feelings cascaded through her just as Pete found his release.

In the sudden stillness of the night, their breaths rasped through the air like a storm. Gradually quiet descended. Liz feared what Pete would say. But he remained silent, speaking only with his hands as he wrapped his arms around her and cuddled her against his chest. She sighed deeply—and fell asleep.

Chapter Sixteen

The early-morning rays of the sun woke Pete the next day. He realized two things at once. He wasn't in his bed at the ranch, and Beth was in his arms.

That awareness brought on a storm of questions. Fortunately his head was clear this morning. Clear enough to recall the most shocking event of the past twenty-four hours.

His discovery that Beth was a virgin.

He could hardly believe it and yet he knew it was true. Last night when he'd plunged into her, he'd felt the resistance. Her tiny cry of pain only confirmed the realization.

But how? Beth had warned him several times not to believe everything printed. He knew that of course, but...a virgin?

Drawing a deep breath, which moved his body more intimately against Beth's, he swallowed a groan, unwilling to wake her just yet. There were too many contradictions to consider. Beth had not been as he'd expected since her arrival. But last night when she'd ridden to his rescue, he'd assumed the rider was one of his cowboys. He closed his eyes to better picture that scene. The rider he'd seen had been relaxed in the saddle, in control of the animal, not rigid, as Beth rode. And yet the rider had been Beth.

And she'd given Diamond a shot with no hesitation, soothing the animal like an expert. She'd even built up the fire skillfully. A princess who built campfires?

Beth stirred again, and Pete tasted her lips, unable to resist the temptation. "Beth? Time to wake up."

She opened her eyes, but she didn't allow her gaze to meet his for more than a second.

"We have a lot to talk about this morning," he murmured.

"No," she said, already reaching for the zipper of the sleeping bag.

His hand closed over hers, stopping her. "Why didn't you tell me?"

"Would you have believed me?" she shot back, bitterness in her voice.

Honesty forced him to say no. "I find it hard to believe even now."

She shoved his hand away and unzipped the bag. "Don't worry about it."

Worry about it? If he understood everything that had happened, he'd be pleased that his bride had saved herself for marriage, for him. But he didn't understand.

"How did you know how to care for Diamond last night?"

Instead of answering him, she was searching for

and putting on the underwear he'd removed so swiftly last night.

"Beth?" he called sharply as she stood and gathered her clothes. Before he could don his briefs, she was out of sight behind the boulders. Hurriedly dressing in the clean clothes Beth had brought him, he then stood waiting for her to reappear.

"I hear a truck," she announced as she rounded the boulders.

He'd picked up the sound, too. As anxious as he was to get help for Diamond, he'd wish for a few more minutes alone with Beth. "Me, too. I guess Harvey was out early."

"He was picking up the vet at four."

"Beth," he said urgently even as the pickup came into view, "we've got some things to talk about. As soon as we get back to the ranch, I want some answers."

She stared at him before packing the saddlebag she'd brought. "I have to leave this morning."

"Not before we talk. There'll be time," he insisted. He'd make sure there was time.

She ignored him, kneeling to roll up the sleeping bag as if she camped frequently. Another question to be answered.

In spite of his questions, however, his body still responded to the sight of her. He'd thought making love to her would lessen his desire, but instead, it had only increased. He reached out and pulled her against him. To his surprise tears filled her eyes.

"Darlin', what—"

To his surprise her lips met his and her hands slid

around his neck. Never one to turn down what he wanted, Pete held her tightly against him, their mouths tasting each other, loving each other.

The sound of a truck horn broke them apart. Pete reluctantly let Beth leave his embrace, but he made a mental note to discover what those tears meant when they had more time.

LIZ FOUGHT BACK the tears as she returned to rolling up the sleeping bag and gathering the saddlebags in which she'd brought the supplies to Pete last night.

She'd made a monumental mistake.

Last night she'd lost her head. It had been impossible to remember the reasons she should keep her distance from Pete. Fear had filled her the entire three-hour ride, fear she wouldn't find him, or if she did, he'd be injured, beyond her help.

When she'd finally seen the campfire in the distance, she'd raced to his side, unable to hold back her feelings for him. That he'd escalated their touching shouldn't have been a surprise. But she'd been unprepared for the emotions that had swamped her.

This morning, however, all the difficulties that would arise from their making love filled her head. In spite of them, she'd taken one more kiss. A goodbye kiss.

"You okay, boss?" Harvey called as the pickup and trailer came to a halt a few feet away.

Liz didn't look up. She wasn't sure she could face anyone this morning. A groan almost escaped her as she realized the hardest people to face would be Petrocelli and Dansky. They had every right to ask for their money back. After all, she'd betrayed the princess with her actions.

"I'm fine, Harvey," Pete responded. "Hi, Doc. I think Diamond made it through the night in pretty good shape. We gave him an antibiotic shot last night."

All three men immediately moved to examine the horse. Liz wished she could slip away while they were occupied, but Beauty, her mount, was tethered beside Diamond.

"Beth, come meet Dr. Grey," Pete called to her.

With a sigh Liz stepped over to Pete's side and extended her hand to the doctor. The man reminded her of her father.

After the amenities were taken care of, Harvey said, "Well, let's get these animals loaded."

"I can ride Beauty back," Liz said. "There's no need to load her."

"Ignore her, Harvey," Pete ordered. Then he turned to Liz. "You're going with me, sweetheart."

"But I have to be back to catch my plane."

"I think you should postpone your trip for at least one more day. But whether you do that or not, you'll be back at the ranch house faster by going with us."

"But there's not enough room in the cab," she protested.

"Sure there is, as long as you sit on my lap," Pete said with a challenging stare, daring her to protest.

Liz couldn't hold back the color that flooded her cheeks.

The three men worked quickly, and before Liz knew it, they were all in the pickup, heading for the ranch. As Pete had suggested, she was seated on his lap, fighting the desire the physical contact filled her with.

Liz figured she deserved such torture. After all, if she hadn't slept with him the night before, she wouldn't know what she'd be missing. She wouldn't be longing for his touch on every inch of her body as she'd felt it last night.

And she wouldn't be feeling so guilty, either.

Since the veterinarian was confident he could stitch up Diamond at the ranch as well as he could at his office, Harvey headed the truck straight for the ranch. In daylight, with the creek almost its normal level, they were able to use a crossing about a mile from where they'd camped. That direct route put them back at the ranch about an hour later.

It was only eight-thirty in the morning, but Liz knew everyone on the ranch would be up. She wasn't going to have long to wait before she faced Petrocelli and Dansky.

Harvey stopped the truck and trailer outside the barn. Pete said to Liz as she slid off his lap to step down, "Go on up to the house, Beth, and get a proper cup of coffee. I'll be there as soon as Doc stitches up Diamond. It shouldn't take more than half an hour. That will still give us a little time to talk before you have to leave—if you still insist on going."

He tried to convey with his gaze what he couldn't say in front of the others. Liz knew he intended to question her again about last night. Hopefully Dansky and Petrocelli would help her avoid that questioning.

She turned to go, but her fingers itched to touch

him again, to stroke that cheek, to feel his rock-hard chest. As if reading her mind, he caught her arm and leaned over to give her a brief kiss. She tried not to cling to him. But it was hard. It was even harder to turn her back on him and walk toward the house.

Before she was halfway there, Petrocelli came out onto the porch. As soon as he saw her, he hastened over to her. "Your Highness, we are glad you returned safely."

"Thank you, Petrocelli. I'm sorry I didn't let you know about...about anything before I left."

Taking her arm, he whispered desperately, "Please hurry. There have been developments."

"Developments?"

"We must go to your room at once. Do not stop in the kitchen to chat."

"But I thought I'd have a cup of coffee and—"

"No."

She looked at him in puzzlement as she stepped onto the porch. What could she do but agree? She'd already caused them more difficulties than they knew. She supposed immediate confession would be the wisest course.

"You're back!" Maisie exclaimed as she walked into the kitchen.

Lady Hereford rose from the table and both women hugged Liz as if she'd just returned from the Crusades.

"I'm fine and so is Pete," she assured them. "He'll be up as soon as the vet has finished working on Diamond."

Petrocelli tugged on her arm. "The princess must

shower.'' Without giving her time to say more, he pulled her from the kitchen.

He didn't speak as they climbed the stairs, and she decided all conversation should take place in her room, behind closed doors.

Swinging open the door, Liz stepped into the room, her mouth open, ready to question her escorts. Then there was no need. Everything suddenly became very clear.

Sitting on the sofa before the fire was a young woman, an almost exact replica of Liz. She rose to her feet as Liz came to an abrupt halt.

Instead of speaking to her, Princess Elsbeth turned to Dansky, raising one eyebrow. ''You thought *she* could replace me?''

''She has been camping, Your Highness. When she is properly groomed, the resemblance is amazing,'' Dansky assured her.

Petrocelli stepped around Liz, closing the door behind him. ''I can assure you, Your Highness, Miss Caine has done an admirable job as your substitute.''

''Very well. Reward her and then send her away.'' The princess sat back down on the sofa and picked up a magazine.

Finally Liz snapped out of her stupor. ''Your Highness, may I—''

''She dares to speak to me?'' the woman said in a cold voice, looking at Dansky.

''Your Highness,'' he replied hurriedly, ''she might want to tell you about her relationship with Lord Peter.''

''Really?'' the princess drawled incredulously. ''I

believe I will manage to sort out any difficulties. After all, I am his fiancée, not her.'' She began flipping pages in the magazine.

''May I take a shower before I am dismissed?'' Liz asked, irritated by the woman's attitude.

''I'm sorry,'' Petrocelli said softly. ''You must leave at once, before Pete returns to the house. It will be for the best, I assure you.''

''But—'' Liz wanted to explain about the difficulties that had arisen since she'd last seen her escorts, but Dansky cut her off.

''No, Miss Caine. No arguments, please. The car is waiting for you downstairs. We have packed the clothing we promised you. Here is money for your ticket. Our alliance is at an end. We ask that you maintain your silence as you promised.''

''But there's something—''

Petrocelli took her arm. ''Even your purse is in the car. Dansky will distract the others while I take you out the front door.''

Liz stared at the three of them. She had grown fond of the two men, but their dismissal of her now, without even offering her the courtesy of listening, lessened the sadness she felt.

The fact that she was leaving Pete, Maisie, Lady Hereford and the entire ranch without having an opportunity to say goodbye was devastating, but she held that sorrow in as she backed out of the room. Petrocelli took the envelope Dansky held out to her.

He followed her from the room, silently going down the stairs with her and out the front door. He swung open the back door of the limousine.

Without looking at him Liz slid into the spacious seat.

"Miss Caine, in spite of the princess's words, you were an able conspirator. We are grateful."

She gave him a brief glance and a half smile. It was all she could muster as she fought to keep the tears at bay.

He dropped the envelope in her lap. "Good-bye...and thank you."

Then he stepped back and closed the door.

The uniformed driver immediately eased the car forward, heading down the long driveway that led to a different life for Liz.

A life that had nothing to do with a sinfully handsome cowboy named Pete.

The tears streamed down her cheeks.

THE VET'S WORK on Diamond took a little longer than Pete expected, and it was almost an hour before he was free to go to the house.

His mother and Maisie greeted him with enthusiasm. After he answered their first questions, he had one of his own. "Where's Beth? Packing?"

"She went up to have a shower," Maisie explained. "And she hasn't come back down."

"I'll grab a hot shower and then bring her down with me. Has their car come for the airport?"

"That's the strange thing. A car came about seven this morning. Dansky went out after the driver knocked on the door and asked for him. And it stayed here until about half an hour ago when it left."

"Left?" Pete echoed, suddenly afraid that Beth had

departed without saying goodbye. Then he took a deep breath. She wouldn't do that. Of course she hadn't gone. But he wanted to check, anyway.

"I'll look in on Beth before I take a shower." Without waiting for a response, he hurried up the stairs.

"Beth?" he called, rapping on her door.

Petrocelli opened the door slightly. "Her Highness is resting."

Pete insisted. "She won't mind me interrupting her. Move aside."

"Her Highness—"

"Let him in, Petrocelli," a cool voice ordered.

Pete frowned as Petrocelli swung open the door, but he was eager to see Beth, so he shoved his doubts aside. She was seated on the sofa in front of the fire, and she didn't move as Pete came toward her.

"Beth, honey, are you all right?"

She was dressed in silk, as she'd been her first couple of days on the ranch. He supposed she had already prepared for her departure. Taking the magazine from her hands, he threw it on the sofa and pulled her to her feet and into his arms.

He scarcely took in her startled look before his lips covered hers.

The kiss didn't last long. She pulled away, a protest on her lips. Pete stared at the familiar face in puzzlement.

"How dare you?" she demanded.

"How dare I what?" he asked slowly, as he registered various sensations that didn't make sense.

She wrinkled her nose in distaste and brushed off

her silk suit. "Approach me without tending to your grooming needs."

Something was wrong. He was reminded of the first time he'd approached Beth, much more disheveled than now. She'd been startled, but not disdainful.

"And I will not be called Beth," she assured him as she stared down her nose, "nor would I allow anyone to use that disgustingly common term 'honey.'"

He opened his mouth to question her words, but she continued before he could speak.

"And most of all, no one, absolutely no one, makes an assault on my person without my permission."

"Look, Beth, we've gotten way beyond these things. I need to talk to you about what happened."

"What happened?" Dansky said, stepping forward.

"It has nothing to do with you, Dansky," Pete said. He had no intention of discussing his sex life with either of Beth's escorts. "Tell them to go away, Beth."

She cocked one eyebrow and stared at him.

"You don't want to have this discussion in front of them, do you?" He challenged her with his words, sure of her answer even if she *was* acting strangely.

"I don't know what you're talking about," she said coolly.

Anger filled him. She thought she could pretend that they hadn't made love? That she hadn't lost her virginity? "Yes, you do. You know what happened in that sleeping bag last night as well as I do. Do you want me to tell them?"

Petrocelli stepped forward. "Pete, perhaps this discussion could wait until you arrive in Cargenia. We really must depart at once.''

"I heard that the car has already gone. Am I to take you to the airport?"

"No, our car will be arriving any minute. The princess must go down and say goodbye to your mother and Miss Maisie. There will be time for long conversations in Cargenia." Petrocelli smiled as if his suggestion was a good one.

"Beth? Ask them to leave the room."

The princess shook her head no and in a bored voice said, "I do not feel like having a discussion."

"Damn it, Beth, this is important!"

"There is our car," Dansky called from across the room. He began grabbing suitcases.

To Pete's astonishment Beth turned to the door as if she would go without even telling him goodbye. Confused, feeling more than ever that something was wrong, he caught her sleeve.

"How dare you?" she demanded. "Dansky, make him unhand me."

Chapter Seventeen

Suddenly Pete knew, though he didn't understand. This was not his Beth. "Take out your contacts."

Petrocelli and Dansky both stepped forward as if to intervene, but he held up a hand.

"Lord Peter," Dansky exclaimed, "it is not— The princess cannot—"

Petrocelli was more direct. "Pete, you should not—"

"I shouldn't because she can't. Right, Petrocelli?" Pete asked, looking at the shorter man. "This isn't the same woman, right?"

The princess sneered at him. "I do not know what you are saying. I do not wear contacts."

"No, I didn't think you did." Pete turned back to Petrocelli. "Explain."

"Pete, I cannot—" Petrocelli broke off, staring at him helplessly.

"Where is she?"

Both men appeared to understand his question, but they didn't answer.

"I am here," the princess said, as if suddenly realizing she had a role to play. "Your fiancée, darling. That is all you need to know."

"No, Princess, that is not all I need to know. I made love last night to Beth. I want to know where she is."

"The woman got above herself," the princess spit out, turning to glare at her henchmen. "Why did you not stop her?"

"Petrocelli?" Pete asked, ignoring the princess. He had no interest in her. "Where is she?"

"She's on her way to the airport, Pete. We meant no harm. But the princess could not come and we feared you would take offense."

"Offense? Offense? You send a woman here to mislead me and thought that would be better than my taking offense?"

"Pete, please, consider what you will be giving up if you dismiss the princess," Dansky said, stepping forward. "You have agreed—"

Pete turned and gave a formal bow to the princess. "Your Highness, I decline your offer of marriage. Please tell your father to seek another alliance." He ignored the rage on her face. "Now, where is Beth?"

THE FALLOUT from Pete's discovery caused quite a ruckus. Lady Hereford, enraged that the princess had tried to dupe her son, told Her Highness in no uncertain terms what she thought of her behavior. The princess attempted to ignore the duchess's words, but her temper threatened to break loose. Fortunately she was able to escape to the limousine that had arrived.

Pete, frantic to find Beth, finally cornered Petrocelli

as Dansky carried the last of the luggage to the car.
"You've got to tell me where she is, Petrocelli."

"I don't know where she is. I do know her real
name, however. Elizabeth Caine. That's all I can tell
you."

"Elizabeth Caine? But where did you hire her?"

"In Hollywood."

Petrocelli escaped his grasp and ran for the limousine.

Pete stood with his hands on his hips, watching it
drive away.

"Well! I cannot believe the princess would do such
an unscrupulous thing," his mother exclaimed, join-
ing him.

"Actually, Mother, it's the first action I have believed since Beth's—Liz's arrival."

"Who is Liz?"

"The woman pretending to be the princess. The
woman I'm going to marry." No matter how long it
took, Pete knew he'd find his princess.

"But she lied to you."

"Not about everything."

"Where is she?"

"I don't know. I'm going to find her, though, and
get an explanation. And then I'm going to marry
her."

"I think you should wait—"

"Mother, I love you, but you have no say in this
decision. You wanted me married, and I'm going to
marry. The choice of bride is mine."

"But she might lie."

Pete smiled as he thought about the woman he'd

spent the past few days with. The woman he'd shared his life with. The woman he'd loved. "No. She won't lie."

He went back in the house to pack. He was flying to Los Angeles today. He had to locate his bride.

"LIZ, HONEY, take a break and have some lemonade," her mother called from the porch.

Liz wiped her forehead with her sleeve and put down the paintbrush she'd been wielding on the side of the house. A cool drink sounded like a good idea.

Her mother handed her a glass and patted the place in the porch swing next to her.

"I'm worried about you, honey. You've worked nonstop ever since you got back. It's almost as if you're unhappy or trying to forget something. Don't you like being home? Do you want to return to Hollywood?"

Liz took a sip of the lemonade, letting it slowly slide down her parched throat, before she answered. "No, Mom, I don't want to return to Hollywood."

"Then what's wrong?"

"You're right. I'm trying to forget…someone."

"He broke your heart?" Her mother accompanied her anxious words with a soft touch.

"Yes, but it's my fault."

"Why? How could it be your fault?"

Liz closed her eyes. How could it be her fault? Because she'd lied to him. And made love to him while he thought she was another woman.

"It's too much to explain. I'll be all right, though."

Her mother patted her arm in silent sympathy. Then

she said, "Jake Harmon down at the feed store called. He said you could start work Monday if you wanted."

Liz knew she should be glad she'd found a job. In Cushing, Kansas, there weren't a lot of jobs available.

But a week ago she'd been a princess.

And she'd made love to Pete.

It was hard to adjust.

"That's good, Mom. I'll call him later."

"I'm afraid you won't be happy at the feed store, Liz. Are you sure you should take the job?"

Liz stared at her surroundings. She missed the grandeur of the mountains, the lushness of the pastures, the brisk activity of the ranch. Kansas was hot, dusty and, worst of all, didn't include Pete.

She attempted a smile. "I'll be fine, Mom."

The sound of a vehicle coming down the paved road near their house didn't evoke any interest from either of them. Her mother's home was on the outskirts of the small town, which had only one main road, and cars passed frequently.

But this one slowed and turned into their driveway.

"Who do we know with a black pickup?" her mother asked.

Liz's head snapped around and she stared in surprise, her heart beating double time.

A tall handsome cowboy got out of the truck and walked toward her, but he didn't have a smile on his face. In fact, he looked grim and determined.

Liz gulped and slowly stood, her gaze never leaving him. "Hi, Pete."

"Howdy, Princess," he drawled.

Her cheeks flamed and she looked away. "You know I'm not... I'm sorry."

"What's going on, Liz?" her mother asked worriedly.

"Allow me to introduce myself, Mrs. Caine," he said gently, drawing a gasp from Liz that he knew her name. "I'm Pete Morris, owner of the Palisades Ranch near Parsons, Montana."

Her mother, always a lady, stepped forward and offered her hand. "How do you do, Mr. Morris. Welcome to our home. Are you a friend of Liz's?"

"You could say that. Would you mind if I spoke with Liz alone?"

"No!" Liz cried. The last thing she wanted was to be alone with the man she loved. The man she'd betrayed.

Ellie Caine looked at Liz, then at Pete. Finally she turned back to her daughter. "I'll be in the house if you need me." Then she walked inside.

"Nice woman," Pete said.

Liz's eyes grew wider, but she changed the subject. "How did you find me?"

"Petrocelli gave me your real name. That Georgia woman in Hollywood was no help, so I hired a private detective. I would've been here sooner if she'd cooperated."

Liz knew she could count on her old employer to keep her hidden. She stared at him, unsure of what to say.

"Aren't you going to ask me to join you on the swing?"

She looked at the confined space behind her, then

at Pete again. Before she could answer, however, he stepped to her side, took her arm and seated her on the swing, then joined her there.

His arm rested on its back, only an inch away from her, and he pushed with his foot to set the swing in motion. The rocking should've been soothing, but Liz's nerves were tight.

"Pete, I'm sorry," she said. "I didn't—"

"Are you?" he interrupted, his voice casual.

"Yes, of course I am! They didn't tell me everything. I didn't know that we were engaged. I mean, you and the princess. I mean, I thought I was pretending to be her for a formal visit. They said it was so she could avoid the press," Liz finished, unable to look at him.

"And when you found out differently?" His fingers stroked the skin of her upper arm, as if his touch was a casual thing.

Desperately she clasped her hands and stared at her lap, unable to meet his gaze. "I'd already taken the money. I protested, but they said no one else could take my place. And I couldn't repay them."

"And when we made love?" he asked gently. "Did you go along because you'd been paid?"

Liz felt as if she'd been stabbed. "How dare you?" she demanded, springing up from the swing. She'd remembered their time together with pain and longing, but she hadn't expected an attack from Pete.

"How dare I?" Pete repeated. He stood, as well. "How do you think I felt when I discovered a different person waiting for me upstairs? When I realized I'd been duped?"

Guilt filled her and she turned her back to him. "I'm sorry," she whispered, fighting to hold back the tears.

"Do you know how long it took me to figure everything out?"

She frowned. His question was unexpected. "No, I don't."

Strong fingers turned her around and he lifted her chin. "About this long," he whispered just before his lips covered hers.

Longing so powerful it almost left her limp filled Liz. Her arms encircled his neck without volition, and she clung to him as he devoured her. When he pulled back, they were both breathing heavily.

"You knew right away?"

"Oh, yeah. Of course, the princess made it easy when she accused me of assaulting her. She didn't respond like you."

"She didn't?" Liz asked, pleased with his response.

"Nope. You always opened to me. She was a stranger."

He had that cocky grin on his face, and Liz lifted a finger to trace the curve of his mouth. Without warning he caught her hand and carried it, palm up, to his lips.

"Pete…" Liz began, but she didn't know what to say. She'd already apologized several times. "Did your mother and the princess get along all right?"

"You could say that."

"Aren't you going to explain?" she asked, frustration rising.

"Do you think you deserve to know?"

Liz pressed her lips together tightly and turned away again. "Probably not."

He wrapped his arms around her, pulling her back to lean against him. "Mother and the princess agreed to disagree. They don't intend to ever speak to each other again."

Liz drew a sharp breath as Pete's lips traveled down her neck, sending shivers all over her body. "Then what are you going to do?"

"Get married."

"Oh. I...I hope you'll be very happy," she said faintly. And that was the truth. But a painful one.

"Me, too. So how long will it take you to pack?"

She shoved her way out of his arms. He wanted her to come to his wedding? Was he being mean on purpose? Or didn't he realize how painful it would be? "I can't come to your wedding!" she exclaimed.

"Well, hell, darlin', that's going to make things a little difficult," he drawled, just as he had when she'd first met him.

She frowned and risked a quick look at him. He wore a teasing grin that made her want to slap him. "What do you mean?"

"It's hard to have a wedding without a bride."

She stared at him, wanting so much to believe what he was implying. But she couldn't. "I can't."

"Why not? Are you saying you don't love me, that our lovemaking meant nothing to you?" He put his arms around her again and tilted her head to him.

Tears filled her eyes. "No, I'm not saying that. But I know you want the ranch, and your mother—"

"Has already given it to me. To compensate for my broken heart over not marrying a princess." He grinned at her and tightened his embrace.

Liz stared at him, not sure if he was being honest. His lips covered hers and suddenly she didn't care. If he wanted her, she was his, ranch or no ranch, princess or no princess.

"Oh, Pete," she cried as he released her lips, "I've missed you so much."

"Me, too, sweetheart. I've wanted to wring your neck a few times, but mostly I want to love you—for the rest of our lives. Can you handle that?"

"Yes," she whispered. "Please, yes."

"That's my princess," he said, and swung her around in his enthusiasm. "Let's go tell your mom. Think she'd like to live in Montana?"

"Oh, Pete," Liz sobbed into his shoulder. She hadn't even thought about leaving her mother, but now she knew it would be difficult. "How did you know?"

He grinned. "I didn't for sure. But if we're going to get started on those babies right away, I figured we'd need all the help we can get."

"Babies?"

"Mother's and Maisie's orders. You don't mind, do you?"

With love in her eyes, she smiled at him as she cupped his cheek. "No, I don't mind at all."

DEBBIE MACOMBER

invites you to the

HEART OF TEXAS

Join Debbie Macomber as she brings you the lives
and loves of the folks in the ranching community
of Promise, Texas.

If you loved Midnight Sons—don't miss
Heart of Texas! A brand-new six-book series
from Debbie Macomber.

Available in February 1998
at your favorite retail store.

Heart of Texas by Debbie Macomber

HARLEQUIN®

Take 4 bestselling love stories FREE

Plus get a FREE surprise gift!

Special Limited-time Offer

Mail to Harlequin Reader Service®

3010 Walden Avenue
P.O. Box 1867
Buffalo, N.Y. 14240-1867

YES! Please send me 4 free Harlequin American Romance® novels and my free surprise gift. Then send me 4 brand-new novels every month, which I will receive months before they appear in bookstores. Bill me at the low price of $3.34 each plus 25¢ delivery and applicable sales tax, if any.* That's the complete price and a savings of over 10% off the cover prices—quite a bargain! I understand that accepting the books and gift places me under no obligation ever to buy any books. I can always return a shipment and cancel at any time. Even if I never buy another book from Harlequin, the 4 free books and the surprise gift are mine to keep forever.

154 HEN CE7C

Name	(PLEASE PRINT)

Address	Apt. No.

City	State	Zip

This offer is limited to one order per household and not valid to present Harlequin American Romance® subscribers. *Terms and prices are subject to change without notice. Sales tax applicable in N.Y.

UAM-696

©1990 Harlequin Enterprises Limited

MEN at WORK

All work and no play? Not these men!

April 1998
KNIGHT SPARKS by Mary Lynn Baxter
Sexy lawman Rance Knight made a career of arresting the bad guys. Somehow, though, he thought policewoman Carly Mitchum was framed. Once they'd uncovered the truth, could Rance let Carly go...or would he make a citizen's arrest?

May 1998
HOODWINKED by Diana Palmer
CEO Jake Edwards donned coveralls and went undercover as a mechanic to find the saboteur in his company. Nothing—or no one—would distract him, not even beautiful secretary Maureen Harris. Jake had to catch the thief—*and* the woman who'd stolen his heart!

June 1998
DEFYING GRAVITY by Rachel Lee
Tim O'Shaughnessy and his business partner, Liz Pennington, had always been close—but never *this* close. As the danger of their assignment escalated, so did their passion. When the job was over, could they ever go back to business as usual?

MEN AT WORK™

Available at your favorite retail outlet!

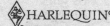 HARLEQUIN®  *Silhouette*®

Look us up on-line at: http://www.romance.net   PMAW1

HARLEQUIN®

A M E R I C A N ◆ R O M A N C E®

COMING NEXT MONTH

#729 WANTED: DADDY by Mollie Molay
Jeremy and Tim knew exactly what kind of father they wanted, but
nothing they did made their mom go out and find him. The boys had no
choice: they had to take matters into their own hands and kidnap a dad!

#730 THE BRIDE TO BE...OR NOT TO BE? by Debbi Rawlins
Showers

Kelly was looking forward to her button-down small-town life with ol'
reliable Gary in their soon-to-be-built new home. So why, then, was the
sexy carpenter igniting her with his searing glances that threatened to
burn down her white picket defenses?

#731 HUSBAND 101 by Jo Leigh
Shy Sara Cabot was assured *Thirty Steps to Sure Success with the Opposite
Sex* would work for anyone. Then she tried them on a hunky ex-navy
SEAL. The steps were guaranteed...but to do what?

#732 FATHER FIGURE by Leandra Logan
Charles Fraser was used to doing his father's bidding, so how bad could
becoming a father figure to his five-year-old nephew really be? But then
he met the boy and his hard-to-resist mom....

AVAILABLE THIS MONTH:

#725 DIAGNOSIS: DADDY
Jule McBride

#727 A BACHELOR FALLS
Karen Toller Whittenburg

#726 A COWBOY AT HEART
Judy Christenberry

#728 A LITTLE BIT PREGNANT
Charlotte Maclay

Look us up on-line at: http://www.romance.net